Hard Riding

Bill Freeman

Algonquin Educational Productions

Toronto 2012

Books and other creative works by Bill Freeman

Adult Non-fiction books

The End of War, 2012
Hamilton: A People's History, 1999
Far from Home: Canadians in the First World War, with Richard Nielsen, 1999
A Magical Place: Toronto Island and Its People, 1999
Casa Loma: Toronto's Fairy-tale Castle and Its Owner, Sir Henry Pellatt, 1998
1005: Political Life in a Union Local, 1982
Their Town: The Mafia, the Media and the Party Machine, with Marsha Hewitt, 1979

The Bains Series of Young Adult Fiction books

Ambush in the Foothills, 2000
Sioux Winter, 1999
Prairie Fire!, 1998
Danger on the Tracks, 1987
Harbour Thieves, 1984
Trouble at Lachine Mill, 1983
First Spring on the Grand Banks, 1978
The Last Voyage of the Scotian, 1976
Shantymen of Cache Lake. 1975

Theatrical Plays

Glory Days: 2007

First performance, Theatre Aquarius, Hamilton, 1989. Remounted by Theatre Aquarius in September/October 2006
Ghosts of the Madawaska: First performance, Great Canadian Theatre Company, 1985

Children's Television Series

Scriptwriter, *Mighty Machines 2* and *Mighty Machines 3*, 28 half-hour programs for preschool children produced for TVO and Treehouse

Television and Educational Videos

Scriptwriter for several documentary television programs and the *Elements of Science*, a series of educational videos produced for the Discovery Educational Network

Awards and Prizes

A Magical Place: Certificate of Commendation, Heritage Toronto, October 2000

Casa Loma: Award of Merit, Heritage Toronto, October 1999

Prairie Fire selected for the Canadian Children's Book Centre "Our Choice" list and nominated for the Geoffrey Bilson Award for Historical Fiction for Young People, 1998

Sioux Winter nominated for the Ontario Library Silver Birch Award, 2000

Several books in the Bains Series were selected for "Our Choice" list.

Vicky Metcalf Award for Children's Literature, 1984 (for a body of work, the Bains Series)

Canada Council Award for Juvenile Literature, 1976

ISBN: paper book: 978-0-9878129-2-6; electronic book: 978-0-9878129-3-3

Design and cover illustration: Baye Hunter
Copyeditor: Lynn Cunningham

Algonquin Educational Productions
3 Seneca Avenue
Toronto, Ontario, Canada
M5J 2A1

Library and Archives Canada Cataloguing in Publication

Freeman, Bill, 1938-
Hard riding / Bill Freeman.

Issued also in an electronic format.
ISBN 978-0-9878129-2-6

I. Title.

PS8611.R432H37 2012 C813'.6 C2012-905776-2

CHAPTER 1

Shadows were lengthening as the evening approached. Shelly was peddling her bike west along College Street, heading home to The Hawk and Baby Marilyn.

She was supposed to work until the nine o'clock closing at the art store on Spadina, but Frank, the owner, had let her leave early because he knew she wanted to get home to her baby. *Such a nice guy*, she said to herself as she peddled her bike. *He's so thoughtful.* Shelly said it over in her mind, and she meant it.

The Hawk, what a silly name for a man, and she smiled to herself, *but it's him.* His real name was Samuel, and she sometimes called him that, but when they were in art school his friends called him The Hawk.

He was in his bad boy phase when Shelly met him at OCAD—Ontario College of Art and Design. His hair was long, and he braided it. Sometimes he even wore a feather. He'd found a leather jacket with fringe on the sleeves in a second-hand store and wore blue jeans and boots laced up to his calf. He was part Indian, and his friends started to call him Mohawk. That made him furious. An insult to my people, he said. So they settled on The Hawk. It suited him.

Back then Hawk filled large canvases with splashes of red and yellow paint. She asked him once why red and yellow? "Those are McDonald's colours, and I'm puking out the fast food all over my canvas." She laughed, but that only ignited more anger.

The Hawk wore his bad boy attitude with pride. Shelly knew that it was partly a put-on. Some saw him as seeking attention, self-centred and full of bluster and ego, but she learned that he was really not like that. All he needed was to be stroked and he turned into the charming little boy who lived inside.

At first she was drawn to him out of curiosity, maybe infatuation. He was different from all the others, and she admired his arrogant determination. But then, after their relationship began, her feelings toward him deepened. She was reluctant to call it love, but in time that was the only word that seemed appropriate.

When the baby arrived, it made a difference in their lives. Now he gave up the rebel pose and was content just to stay at home day and night. He worked constantly. Shelly had never seen anyone so driven to succeed.

The College Street ride was good that night. It was a warm evening, but there was a smell of fall in the air. People were in the bars and restaurants. She could hear laughter and hints of music. This was her neighbourhood, and she loved the feel and texture of it. At Clinton the outdoor section of the Italian restaurant was filled to overflowing with people waiting on the street for a table. Before the baby, that had been one of their favourite haunts.

Shelly was in love with city life. She was from the burbs. Mississauga. Her parents had been afraid for her safety when she told them she was going to go to OCAD and live downtown. They still probably worried about her, but it was too late now. She would never live anywhere else.

As she rode along she wondered what choices her Baby Marilyn would make in her life. They named her Marilyn because that was her mother's name. She remembered the moment she told her mother that they had chosen that name for the baby, and her mother burst into tears out of sheer joy. That was the least Shelly could do. Her parents had given her so much and had been so generous.

Even when she told them that she was pregnant and was going to marry The Hawk, they didn't criticize. She knew that they did not like him because he acted the rebel boy when they were around. It was hard for them. Her parents lived in a middle-class, four-bedroom house and drove new cars. Her father sold insurance, after all.

But after the baby came The Hawk changed, or he tried to change, at least. She gave him credit for that. When they were going out to visit her parents in Mississauga he would read *The Globe and Mail* and make an effort to talk about politics with her father.

After one of those visits he said, "You know, your father knows a lot about politics." She smiled at the thought of it, but he went on, "I don't know how he can believe all of that crap about why we have to fight a war in Afghanistan."

She didn't say anything—that was what The Hawk was like. But even his art was changing. He didn't paint the big, extravagant canvases anymore. "It's a waste of paint," he had said recently. Now he was painfully crafting stylized images of imaginary animals with bold, vivid colours. They were dream-like, idealized, strikingly simple figures. In the bottom right corner of each painting he finished he drew the image of a hawk—his mark.

It was like he was trying to bridge the two parts of himself, the Aboriginal and the European. He told her he needed to cut away the meaningless stuff and find what really matters inside. He was beginning to sell some of his work. A friend had promised to give him a show in his gallery.

Shelly had put her own art aside and was working in the art shop on Spadina to support all three of them while Hawk honed his skill and pursued his vision. For now that was enough for her. Once the baby had come, it seemed that all her passion for her own art had vanished.

She had studied costume design. As a little girl she had gone to the theatre with her mother, and when the curtain went up, the magic of the theatrical world captured her. She loved the outrageous in theatre and dreamed that she could create her own vision. That's why she went to OCAD, but now it was gone. The Hawk possessed her body and soul, and there was little left for her now that the baby had come, and he was in the full flush of his talent.

Sometimes she wondered about that. Had she given in to his selfish demands too much? Had she allowed him to occupy her mind and her body and her life to the point that there was little left over for her creativity? But did it really matter? Baby Marilyn and The Hawk filled her life.

She didn't want to think about that now. As she peddled along, she held in her mind all of the riches that the College Street world had given her. The neighbourhood, The Hawk, Baby Marilyn—this was her life now, and she loved and nurtured it.

Soon she would be home, and the baby would greet her with a big smile. Baby Marilyn would call out and gurgle and coo with excitement. She would stand up in her crib and stamp her feet. The Hawk would put down his paintbrush and get up from his work table. He would laugh and call out to her, "Shelly! Shelly! We're here, Shelly! Welcome home, darling!" And he would sweep her up in his arms. What more could a woman want from life?

A big SUV was driving recklessly up ahead. It would speed up and then fall back. Then it crowded into the bike lane. It was a big, dark, muscular vehicle full of power. The SUV drove up to a red light and stopped. Shelly came up beside it and glided to a halt, waiting for the light to change.

She looked in the window and could see the driver. His shoulders and arms encircled the steering wheel as if all of his energy were focused there. There was a tenseness about him. His blond hair was cut short and stood up like a brush cut. The face of the driver was a baby pink that looked soft and chubby like an overfed infant's, only he was fat. She caught sight of his double chin hanging loose with flesh.

Just then a courier came up behind her, riding fast, peddling hard. He paused at the light to shout at the man in the SUV.

"Keep over! You're crowding into the bike lane," he yelled. People on the street stopped to look and listen.

The courier hesitated for a moment at the red light and then went through the intersection. The driver in the SUV rolled down the window on the passenger side. "Asshole!" he shouted at the disappearing cyclist.

Shelly waited. The driver of the SUV seemed in a panic and didn't know what to do. The light was green, and a driver in the line behind honked his horn. Suddenly the SUV launched ahead, narrowly missing a pedestrian. Shelly followed cautiously behind.

She could hear the squeal of brakes up ahead. The SUV had stopped half in the bike lane, half in the vehicle lane, blocking the courier. They were shouting at each other. "You're crowding the bike lane!" she could hear the courier say. Now he was leaning his bike against a lamppost.

Shelly came to a stop. Other cyclists came up behind her and stopped as well. They were not going to get involved.

The courier walked behind the SUV. There were more shouts. Cars were honking, unable to get past. Suddenly, the SUV jumped ahead. It went up on the sidewalk. Tires squealed. Dust flew. Then it lurched back onto the road. The driver sped ahead, but braked hard to keep from ramming the other cars waiting at the Dovercourt stoplight.

The courier looked stunned for a moment, but then he went to his bike, put it back on the path and continued. Shelly followed, and the other riders trailed out behind her.

As they neared the intersection, the courier did an abrupt turn behind the SUV and rode across the street and disappeared. He didn't want any more to do with this.

Shelly rode cautiously up to the corner. The light had changed, and the cars were going through the intersection. It was a downward slope. Her bike gathered speed. She peddled hard to get across before the light changed.

In an instant, the SUV turned a hard right across her path. Her front wheel slammed into the side of the car. She was thrown forward under the car, and the large right back tire rode over her.

CHAPTER 2

He could feel the engine humming. Two hundred horsepower, smooth like the purring of a cat ready to leap forward with the touch of the pedal. It was a SUV, biggest in the lot, with extra-large tires and reinforced suspension. Nothing could stop him.

Driving along College Street in early October the windows were up, and the radio was playing the golden oldies. He was sealed inside, feeling like the outlaw riding into town in one of those old cowboy movies.

It was a warm Friday evening. Traffic was thickening. There were crowds in the restaurants and bars and people gathered on the street. Women, men, old and young—they were milling about laughing and joking as they shared the gossip of their community.

Losers, he thought. *Wops, Eyeties. Talking in their own language 'cause they don't even know English. Women with their fuckin' cleavage so low you could see their fuckin' navel.*

He smiled at the thought. That's what he had said to his brother Ricky just the other day. They were out in the plant watching the workers assemble the refrigeration units. "Fuckin' immigrants don't know if their ass is punched or bored," he had said.

Yeah, that's it. Their women are just waitin' to get laid. His car rolled to a stop at a red light. He stirred a bit at the thought of women and peered out through the window at a group standing at the street corner.

Maybe he'd get himself one tonight. They don't cost much. He could afford it. The bills were lying crisp and clean in his wallet—lots of them—ready to be spent. *Money can buy anything in this town,* he thought.

As he waited for the light to change, a cyclist in the bicycle lane on the right-hand side of his car came up to the corner, hesitated for a moment and then went through the red light.

Fuckin' bastards don't obey the traffic laws. They're worse than the fuckin' foreigners.

The cyclist sped down the street. He was a tall, thin guy, lean and fit, with no helmet, his long hair blowing in the wind. He hated guys like that. *Probably a fuckin' hippie with no respect for the laws.* The cyclist was almost down at the next corner before the light changed, but he'd catch the son of a bitch.

He floored the SUV and the tires squealed. People on the street stopped talking to look at him. His big car lurched forward, eager to catch up, but just then another vehicle pulled out into his lane, and he had to brake. *Lost him,* and the driver swore again.

Ricky wouldn't take shit from a guy like that. No way. Ricky's cool—knows how to handle things. It was Ricky who brought me into the business. He didn't have to do that. That's what brothers are for. They look after their own family. But then he must have known that I was a good salesman, talking to the customers and all that stuff, telling jokes. That gets them on the hook. That's what Ricky says.

It was all getting better since he left his wife. *Fuckin' bitch.* Best thing he ever did was to get out. *Goddamned women. They just want to put you down. You're drinking too much. Why don't you lose some weight? Get a good job. If it wasn't for your brother you'd be nothing. That's what she said to him. Goddamn her anyway.*

He hated all that. It reminded him of all those punks when he was a kid. *Fatso,* they called him and laughed. Well, he showed them. *Fuckin' bastards!* He'd like them to see him now, sitting in his office, answering the phone, going out to lunch with Ricky and talking about refrigeration units.

He didn't need her anyway. *Bitch! She takes all my goddamned money. All she does is sit around at home talking on the fuckin' phone with those lazy friends of hers. I bet some guy's pokin' her right now. I wouldn't be surprised. And on my money, too! Fuckin' bitch. Never did a day's work in her goddamned life, just lived off me. That's all. Bitch!*

He came up behind a line of cars waiting for a streetcar and had to stop while people got on and off. "Hurry up, for Christ's sake!" he shouted out loud. "You just fuck up the whole traffic! Bike lanes on either side that take out two lanes of traffic. Goddamn streetcar in the middle. There's no room for the cars! Jesus, roads are for cars and trucks! Not fucking bicycles or streetcars!" But no one could hear him.

He steered over into the bike lane, trying to see past the streetcar. Bikes flashed by on his right-hand side. "Get off the fuckin' road!" the driver shouted into the darkened car.

Maybe I should cruise over to Yonge Street. There's bound to be some girls up around Wellesley. No, it's too early yet. Maybe another cold beer in one of these bars. No, almost got it the last time. Ricky got me out of that one. It was fuckin' close.

He was the first car behind the streetcar now and it took an eternity. Palmerston, Clinton, Montrose—every stop he had to brake and wait while the people got off. People coming home from work on a Friday night. *What do they know? Can't even afford a car. Gotta ride the stupid streetcar. They should be banned. All they do is fuck up traffic.*

Between stops, when the streetcar picked up speed, the driver tried to get past on the right-hand side. He would steer his big car over toward the curb, into the bike lane, trying to see past the lumbering streetcar. Finally he managed to get around it by dodging into the bike lane and accelerating hard until he was past and into the open lane again.

But the traffic was slow. All the cyclists were bunching up now. They passed him in the bicycle lane: one, two, then a half-dozen or more, one right after the other. *Scruff—not one of them decently dressed. Fuckin' losers! Never had a job, I bet. Should send them out to a labour camp or somethin'. Let them work for a living. Fuckin' assholes.* The anger boiled up in him.

Once he had to go up to York University, and he saw all of them sitting around in the students' mall. *Just sittin' there all day doin' nothin' but talk, talk, talk. Never did any work. Those losers wouldn't know how to work.*

He came to a stop at a red light. A cyclist came up beside him. He was shouting at him. "What the fuck did you say?" the driver replied, but he couldn't be heard. He powered down the window on the passenger's side and was about to say something, but the cyclist rode through the red light. "Asshole!" he shouted at the disappearing cyclist.

Then the light turned green. For a moment he was confused. What to do? There was a honk from someone behind him. He floored it, and the big SUV leapt forward, narrowly missing someone crossing at the light. *Fucker made me look stupid!*

That's the son of a bitch. He could see the cyclist up ahead, peddling hard along the bike path, but his big car was faster. In a moment he was up to him—young, a week's stubble on his face, a courier bag slung over his shoulders, legs like tree trunks, lean and fit.

The driver powered down his window. "What'd you say to me?" he shouted at the courier.

The courier slowed when he heard him. The SUV drove past, and the driver turned the car so the front of the SUV went across the bicycle lane. The courier had to brake hard to avoid hitting the side of the car.

"Watch what you're doing!"

"What the fuck did you say to me back there?" the driver shouted out of the window.

"I said get over! Three times you drove into the bike lane!"

"Fuck off, you shit!"

"It's a bike lane!"

"It's a fuckin' road! It's got cars on it, for fuck's sake! Roads are made for cars, not bicycles!"

"Move your car! You're blocking the bike lane! There's bikes coming behind!" The courier got off his bike and leaned it up against a lamppost. He looked angry.

The front of the big SUV was across the bike lane, and the rear end stuck out over the traffic lane blocking cars. A driver was honking his horn at him.

The courier was walking around behind his car, coming over to the driver's side. He was tall, bunched up muscles in his shoulders, flat stomach—fit from the constant bike riding. He had a tattoo on his neck. His face looked dark and threatening. Panic. The guy was going to yank open the car door and get after him. Pull him out of the car. Smash his face. His heart pounded. *Holy fuckin' Christ!*

The courier was at his window, shouting. "Keep your car off the bike lane! Someone could get hurt!"

The driver floored it. The big car lurched forward and bumped up over the curb. Frantically, he pulled at the wheel. Tires shrieked, dust from the margin spewed out behind. He had to fight with the wheel to bring the SUV back onto the road again. He sped down the street, his heart pounding. Suddenly, he had to brake to keep from banging into the cars lined up, waiting for the Dovercourt stoplight. He powered up all the windows to feel safe. Then he looked in his mirror.

The courier was still in the street, stunned. He seemed to gather himself together, and he walked over to get his bike. Was he going to come for him again? Was he? *I'll teach the fuckin' asshole. Jesus, anarchist sons of bitches.* The courier was getting on his bike. *He's comin' for me.* The courier was coming up the bike path. A whole line of cyclists was following him, strung out, one after the other, pumping hard, gathering speed.

Now the driver was breathing heavily, panting. His heart pounded. "Move!" he shouted at the cars ahead of him. "Move, for fuck's sake!"

The courier was in the bike lane, just behind him. The driver could see him in the big mirror on the right-hand side of the SUV. *I'll show the son of a bitch. He's not gonna get me. Who the fuck is he anyway? Who the fuck does he think he is?*

The light had changed. The cars up ahead were moving through the intersection. The SUV clung close to the back bumper of the one ahead. They were coming up to the corner. The courier was just at his back wheel. *I'll get the fucker! I'll get the fuckin' loser!*

He was at the corner. The driver pulled a sudden hard right across the bike lane. He heard a bump on the side of his car, and felt his right back tire as it rode up and over something.

CHAPTER 3

Mariner was at his desk working on his paperwork when the call came. "This is Dispatch. There's been an accident at College and Dovercourt. A cyclist is down. Crowd is gathering. Officer on the scene is calling for backup. Ambulance has been called. Fourteen Division is short staffed and needs help."

He hung up the phone. "Let's go, Alex," the detective said to his partner. They were expecting action. It was a Friday evening when things always happened.

They grabbed their jackets, took the keys for one of the cruisers parked out front and were out the door.

Alex took the wheel. "Should I use the siren?" He was the junior man. In the police world, the senior officer always made the decisions.

"Yeah. Someone's down."

They headed west from 52 Division headquarters on Dundas Street with the siren wailing and the lights flashing. Cars scattered on both sides as they sped by.

The police radio came to life. "I need backup! Backup! I'm at College and Dovercourt. A cyclist is down. Crowd...." and the voice of the policeman went silent.

Alex drove in the centre of the street, dodging through the traffic. They both were tense, watching, expecting the worse.

"Head up Beverly," Mainer ordered. He tried to sound calm, but his heart was pounding. He hated the high speed in the downtown. When he was in uniform, he had been involved in an accident in a chase. He was laid up for a week and still had a bad knee from it.

Darcy, Baldwin, Cecil—they barely slowed at each corner. A guy on a bicycle ran up on the sidewalk to get out of their way. At College they went through the red light and turned left. At Spadina they were forced almost to a stop as the cars dodged out of the way. Then Alex floored it again. The flashing lights reflected in the storefront windows as they passed. An echo from the siren came back to them from the tall buildings. At the Bathurst light it was the same.

As they sped down the centre of College Street, cars pulled over into the bike lanes. Cyclists stopped to watch. People came out of the bars and restaurants, cursing the cops for disturbing the peace of the night.

The intersection of College and Dovercourt was clogged with traffic in all four directions. There were flashing lights of a police car at the northeast corner that had pulled in front of a big SUV, blocking its escape. A large crowd of people was gathered on the sidewalk.

Alex took the corner and pulled in beside the other police car. He turned off the wailer and lights. A moment later, they were on the street.

A young policeman was standing in front of an overweight, pink-faced man, protecting him from a group of angry young people. Some were shouting. The detective noticed the legs of what appeared to be a woman lying face down on the pavement just behind the right back tire of the SUV.

Mariner was the senior man, and he took command. "All right! All right! Back off now!" he shouted to the crowd. He held up his badge so all could see. "I am Detective Mariner. Calm down, please! Calm down!"

"He did it to her!" someone shouted.

"Go to hell!" the pink-faced man yelled back.

"He turned right in front of her!"

"Damned drivers!"

"Piss off, will you? Think you own the fuckin' street!" The man was taunting the crowd, contributing to the anger.

"Are you the driver?" Mariner demanded.

"Yeah."

"Be quiet. Go stand by the police cruiser." He turned to his partner. "Alex…." He didn't have to say any more. The plain-clothes policeman took the man's arm and firmly moved him away from the crowd.

Just then another police cruiser arrived. Two uniformed men joined them. By the sound, another car was close by. Every man in the district would respond to a "need backup" call.

Mariner knew both of the officers, and he turned to one of them. "Send a message that everything is under control. Call off the others and ask for someone from traffic to come." The policeman nodded and went back to his car to make the call.

Mariner turned to the other officer. "Go and stand by that guy," and he nodded at the pink-faced man.

"Did he do it?"

"Think so."

Now that authority had been established, the crowd was settling down and talking to each other. A group of cyclists that had witnessed the accident was telling the others what they had seen. There was still anger in the crowd. The young policeman who was first at the scene was standing watching over them uneasily.

"You alone?" Mariner asked.

"Yeah. I needed backup."

The detective nodded. Why did they send a young, uniformed officer out in a police car by himself on a Friday night? They were just asking for trouble. "You did the right thing," and he touched the policeman's shoulder to give reassurance. "Keep them here. Don't let any of the witnesses leave."

Mariner looked back at the driver. He was leaning up against the police cruiser. He was agitated and hostile but frightened all at the same time.

Then the detective went over to look at the car and the damage it had caused. The SUV was in the curb lane of the intersection. It had made a tight right turn from College onto Dovercourt right across the bike lane. There was a dent in the side panel of the car where the bike had hit it.

The victim's bicycle lay in the middle of the bike lane, its front wheel bent from the impact and its spokes broken. The force must have been powerful to bend the wheel like that, he thought. The front light of the bike attached to the handlebars was still on and cast a white light under the car. A red light attached to the seat was still blinking. A small, fashionable handbag was in the wire basket attached to the handlebars. Mariner picked it up, and was about to look inside to find identification, but then he paused to look at the body.

He crouched down on his knees to get a better look. It was not a pretty sight. The right back wheel of the SUV had rolled over the victim's head, crushing it. What remained of her helmet were a few pieces of smashed plastic. Nothing could have saved her from the weight of the car. She would have been killed in an instant. It was a young woman, probably no more than 25.

Mariner thought of his own daughter. Was she out riding her bike on some dangerous street in the city? He felt a shudder go through his body.

This was what he hated about the job. The sudden death of an innocent person, especially one so young; it was almost more than he could bear. For a moment he thought he would tear up, and he fought against it. He didn't want the younger officers to see. Then he felt a sudden spasm in his stomach and a shudder in his shoulders.

"Are you okay?" It was his partner, Alex.

He nodded his head. He knew Alex would understand. "Get a blanket," he said quietly. "No one should die in the road like this."

"The ambulance will be here soon. Traffic is on its way."

Mariner nodded. The detective was in his mid-40s, fit , street smart and experienced in the way of the police. As he moved about the scene he projected a sense of authority.

It took a moment for Mariner to clear his head. Then he walked over to the two policemen watching over the crowd of people that was still gathering. He spoke to the young officer who had been first on the scene. "Get the names and addresses of everyone who witnessed the accident. I want to talk to them. Tell them they are required to stay. Understand?"

"Yes, sir." The young officer replied. Mariner knew he could rely on this one.

He waited for Alex to put the blanket over the body, and then the two of them went to talk to the pink-faced, overweight man.

"You the driver of the SUV?" he asked simply.

"Yeah."

"Driver's licence, please."

The man pulled out his wallet and began fishing through it. "She slammed into me, you know. Christ, there was nothin' I could have done."

He handed the detective his plasticized card. Mariner studied the photo on the card for a moment. It was him, all right. Same round face, same slightly hostile look. Charles Ringate Abbott was the name on the card. The address was a street in North York.

Mariner called over one of the officers and handed him the card. "Run it through the computer." The policeman disappeared into his car.

Alex had taken out his notebook and a pen. He wrote the date, time and location at the top of the page. The rule was record everything. It might be needed in court. Then Mariner began.

"This is an interrogation, Mr. Abbott. What you say could be used against you."

"You gonna charge me with somethin'?"

"I don't know."

"I want a lawyer. I've got my rights."

"You want to tell me anything about the accident?"

"I just turned the corner. I mean, fuck, I couldn't see her."

"She had a light on her handlebars, a red blinking light on the seat and was wearing a light jacket."

"I mean, Jesus, the bikes are thick around here. I couldn't see that little light. I mean, Christ, it was her own fault." He was getting red in the face. Anger or frustration was just below the surface.

The officer came back with the driver's licence in his hand. He whispered in Mariner's ear. "He's had two driving convictions. One is a conviction for drunk driving."

The detective nodded. That was it. If he was over the limit, he was going straight to the slammer. He turned back to the driver.

"Have you had a drink tonight?"

"No, Jesus, what is this?"

The driver's hostility annoyed him. "A person has been killed!"

"But it's not my fault, goddamn it. I was just turning the fuckin' corner and then slam—right into the side of my car. What could I do?"

Mariner suddenly walked away. Traffic had arrived, and he went to one of the officers as he stepped out of the car. "You got a breathalyzer?"

"Yeah."

"Give him a test."

"Did he do it?"

"Just give him the test."

"Okay."

Abbott was trying to convince Alex of his innocence. "What the fuck could I do? It was an accident." His anger and frustration were getting the better of him. "I mean, you cops never chase after the bike riders, do you? Only the drivers of cars."

"Your car killed the girl! That's the difference." Mariner glared at him for a moment before he could continue. "Now, I want you to go and take a breathalyzer test."

"A breathalyzer? Jesus Christ, it's like you're accusing me of somethin' already and all I did was turn the fuckin' corner."

"I want you to have a breathalyzer test."

"I told you I didn't have a drink."

"Then the test will prove your innocence."

"My innocence? For Christ's sake. You just want to rig some fuckin' evidence against me. I didn't have a drink!"

"Prove it to me."

"I'm not taking the fuckin' thing!"

Mariner struggled to control himself. "You are not required by law to do it, but if you refuse it may be used against you."

"You've got the fuckin' thing rigged."

"It's your choice." Mariner waited.

Abbott was uncertain what to do. "What if I don't?"

"Then you are going to jail right now. The lawyers can sort it out."

"You fucker!" Abbott made a sudden motion as if he was going to lunge at Mariner. The other officers responded, ready to grab him. Mariner didn't flinch. He almost enjoyed the moment.

"What's the charge?"

"Drunk driving. Dangerous driving. Maybe more."

"Bastard!"

"It's your choice. Are you going to take the test or not?"

"I've got no fuckin' rights. It's a goddamn police state. All right, I'll take the fuckin' test."

"Okay. Good."

The traffic officer led him away and put him in the backseat of his cruiser.

Mariner's whole body was trembling. He thought for a moment that he might be sick. Alex put his hand on his shoulder, giving the message that he understood the emotional pain that his partner was suffering. Mariner breathed deeply, letting out the air slowly until he regained control. It was getting worse. He was a senior police officer and supposed to be objective, cool and analytical—not let his emotions take over. He was concerned what the young policemen would think.

An ambulance had pulled up alongside the police cars, and two young paramedics were waiting to talk to him.

"What happened?" one asked.

"She's dead," was all Mariner could think to say.

"How?"

"She hit the side of the car with her bike and went over the handlebars. The back wheel of the car ran over her head."

"Christ. There's been too many cyclists hit this year."

"For sure."

"Want us to take her?"

"We've got to get the photos first. The traffic officer's doing the breathalyzer. Then he'll do the photos. After that, she's yours."

"God, you've got to be careful in this town. I ride a bike to work every day."

The paramedic was a young, fit, good-looking guy. Mariner had never met him before, but he knew he liked him. They waited for the traffic officer to finish the test. It took a minute, and then he got out of the police car, leaving Abbott locked in the backseat of the car. He came across to Mariner.

"He registered .03. That's not enough to hold him."

"How much is it?"

"One drink. Maybe two."

Mariner nodded. A drunk driving charge would have been clean and simple. With Abbott's past record, he'd end in jail for sure. "Did you tell him what he registered?"

"No."

"Put him in the backseat of our cruiser. Let him sweat a bit. I want you to take photos. Do the works. She's a young woman. She deserves the best."

The traffic officer nodded and hurried away. He transferred Abbott to Mariner's cruiser, got his camera and began taking photos of the scene.

The detectives talked quietly. "What's her name?" Alex asked and nodded at the purse that was still in Mariner's hand.

"You take a look," Mariner said handing the purse to his partner. To him it seemed like a violation of the dead woman to go through her private effects. Maybe he would tear up again if he saw the details of her life.

There was more work to do. He went across to the young policemen still standing by the large crowd. Mariner asked if he had a list of witnesses. The officer handed him a piece of paper. There were three names with addresses and phone numbers. Mariner chose the first one on the list.

"John Metcalfe," he asked in a loud voice. A tall man of maybe 30 nodded. He was holding a bicycle and wearing a helmet. "I would like to talk to you, please."

He led Metcalfe over toward the police cars so others in the crowd could not hear. Alex stood beside him taking notes, saying nothing.

"Could you tell me carefully, in your own words, what you saw of the accident?"

Metcalfe was upset, but he seemed calm enough. "The car turned right in front of her. She didn't have a chance. I was riding a little behind her, and I saw everything. The light was green, and she was building speed to get across before it turned red, and he turned right in front of her. She slammed into the side of the car and went over the handlebars under the car. God, it was awful. I saw everything. The wheel ran over her head."

"Could she have stopped in time?"

"No. I was behind her, and I had to slam on my brakes. I was barely able to stop."

"Did the driver put on his indicator signal?"

"It all happened so fast. I don't think so."

"It's important. Try to think back."

"I don't think so, but I can't be sure. But you know, there was another thing."

"What's that?"

"The driver had an argument with a courier."

"When?"

"Just before the accident happened. I was riding west on my bike, coming home from work, when I noticed this big car." He pointed at the SUV. "It was at a stoplight back there. This guy, he looked like a courier, was in a shouting match with the driver."

"Is he here?"

Metcalf looked around. "I don't see him, but I'm sure he was a bike courier. He had one of those plastic bike courier bags slung over his back."

Mariner nodded.

"The courier was mad. I could see that, and he shouted at the driver. "

"What did he say?"

"Something about the car coming into the bike lane. I'm not sure. Then he took off through the red light. So the SUV raced after him and drove into the bike lane, blocking the courier. I held back. They were shouting at each other. The courier got off his bike. It looked like there might be a punch-up or something."

"What was he mad about?"

"Like I said, the courier was saying he had come into the bike lane and could have hit someone. That's what it was about."

"Did you see the car come into the bicycle lane?"

"No. He was up ahead of me."

"What about the girl?"

"She was riding ahead of me. I saw her. But she didn't get involved in any of this. In fact, she stopped and waited, just like me."

"Waited for what?"

"Till the argument was over. Like she was just minding her own business. That's all she was doing, and then after it was over, she started riding again. It's a bit of a downhill run, and she was going faster. I could see that. She was getting up speed to get across the intersection before the light changed, and then this guy in the car.... Like, he just turned right in front of her. She didn't have a chance. God, I saw the whole thing. I heard the bump. It was sickening. I threw down my bike, and I ran, but there was nothing I could do. She was dead. There was blood all over. Her head.... I'll never forget it."

"How fast was the car going?"

"I don't know. Suddenly he just swerved right in front of her. Even if she hit her brakes, she couldn't have saved herself. It was just a screech of tires, and wham, and she was under the car. It happened so fast. And you know she didn't make a sound, not a scream, nothing, just that awful, sickening bump of the wheel going over her."

"Did you touch the body?"

"No, I phoned 911 right away on my cell phone."

"Did anyone else touch the body?"

"No, I would have seen it. I told people to stand back. Just to see a young woman like that. Killed! Right in front of me, killed. But then some of the cyclists got into an argument with him. They saw it, too. I mean, you can understand why. He drove right over her. They were furious. It was his fault."

Mariner nodded. Metcalfe was upset, and he wanted to reach out to console him, but it was not the thing a policeman should do. "Is there anything else you want to tell me?"

"I mean, that guy shouldn't have been driving like that. I don't care what anyone says. That girl didn't have to die. Not die like that with her head under the back wheel...." His voice trailed off.

"Thank you, Mr. Metcalfe. We have your name and address and phone number. We'll have you come down to the station and make a statement."

"Yeah, sure, anything. I mean, these guys who drive cars—they've got to know about cyclists. You've got to make them listen."

"Thank you. We'll talk later." Metcalfe went back to the others in the crowd.

Mariner turned to Alex. "Who was this guy who got into an argument with Abbott?"

"Don't know."

"We've got to find him."

The photography was finished and the paramedics were carefully lifting the body onto a stretcher, making sure the blanket covered the terrible sight.

"I looked in her purse," Alex said. "She lives close by. Maybe we should go and tell the family before they find out another way."

"Let's talk to the other witnesses first and then we'll go over."

But by then it was too late to inform the family.

CHAPTER 4

The Hawk was at home, waiting for Shelly. He had fed the baby, and she was crawling on the floor, turning over the coloured plastic blocks that her grandparents had given her.

He was looking forward to having his wife at home. She had phoned to say that she had been let off work early. It was Friday night, and they would have a nice, quiet evening together.

He had so much to tell her about his work. It was going well. It was like everything was finally coming together. Soon he would have enough art that he could have the gallery showing that he had been promised. An editor from *Canadian Art* magazine loved his graphic designs of animals. He even had some ideas he could adapt for the internet.

It seemed like ideas were exploding inside him. He was confident that soon he would be able to support Shelly and the baby with his work. She could do his marketing. Believers were always the best marketers.

And then he got the phone call. It was their friend Derrick on his mobile phone. "Hawk, you're going to have to come down here."

"What?"

"It's Shelly. She's been in an accident."

"Accident?"

"A terrible accident."

"Is she okay?"

"You've got to come down here, Hawk. It's Dovercourt and College. I'll wait for you."

"What's it about?"

"Just come down!" And then The Hawk could tell that Derrick was crying.

He felt a cold panic. "Derrick!" he shouted into the phone, but it was dead. He stood, looking into the phone for a long moment, trying to comprehend what all this meant. Then he began to move quickly and decisively.

Fear gave a sharp clarity to his actions. This was serious. First, he took the baby along the hall to Mrs. Stewart. Then he ran down the apartment hallway, down the steps, unlocked his bike and he rode, rode, rode, his heart pounding, but his mind in clear, sharp focus. Shelly was in an accident, and he had to get to her.

As he came up to the Dovercourt-College intersection and saw the police cars and the ambulance, he knew the worst had happened and with that realization he lost any sense of clarity and was overwhelmed. "Shelly!" he called. "Shelly! Shelly!"

Derrick was there for him. "Oh, Hawk!" was all he could say.

The Hawk dropped his bike, and in the confusion Derrick picked it up. Hawk pushed his way through the crowd.

The onlookers resisted. "Hey!" "Watch out what you're doing!" But he bulled his way through, and when they saw his distress they backed off.

Then he saw it. Shelly's crumpled bike, the two paramedics carrying the stretcher, with a blanket covering something.

"Shelly!" he screamed and ran toward the stretcher. Mariner and Alex both reacted and caught The Hawk in mid-flight.

The blanket covered everything, but Hawk knew it was Shelly, and he knew in that instant—that very moment—that his life and the life of Baby Marilyn had changed forever.

The policemen strained against the powerful young man. "Settle down!" someone said. "Stop it!"

"That's Shelly! It's her! I know it is."

"Is that your wife?" Mariner had both of his arms wrapped around The Hawk's shoulders. "Is it your wife?" he repeated.

Hawk slumped to the sidewalk. All of his energy, all of his fight, had gone out of him. Derrick was there with him now. The two police detectives were kneeling beside him. The large crowd watched the tragedy, but no one could console him. Shelly was dead. What more was there for him? Shelly was dead.

"Are you his friend?" Mariner asked.

"Yes," answered Derrick.

"I think you should come."

Derrick got to his feet, leaving The Hawk slumped on the pavement waiting, waiting for the sentence that would change the rest of his life.

Mariner led Derrick across to the stretcher, which had been put in the back of the ambulance. The two paramedics waited. Everyone waited.

"I am not going to show you her head," Mariner said quietly.

Derrick nodded. "I saw her lying on the ground. It's Shelly and that's The Hawk. It's…it's her man, her partner, her husband. I was with them at art school."

But Mariner needed a positive identification. He pulled back the blanket to show the legs and torso.

"It's her. I know her like she was my sister."

Mariner carefully replaced the blanket. "What's her full name?"

"Shelly McTavish. She didn't take on The Hawk's name when they were married." The talking seemed to calm Derrick.

"Who's The Hawk?"

"It's him," and Derrick nodded in Hawk's direction. "That's what we called him in school. He was the best artist in our class. The very best," and then Derrick began crying again.

"You're going to have to tell him," the policeman was saying.

And Derrick nodded. He knew he had to do it, do it for Shelly and do it for The Hawk. The task gave him purpose, and he was able to collect himself. He went to The Hawk and sank down on his knees beside him.

"It's her, isn't it?" The Hawk said quietly, so softly that Derrick could barely make out what he had said.

"Yes."

"Is it bad?"

"Yeah."

"Can I see her?"

"Maybe later, Hawk, would be best."

"I've got to see her."

"Later."

"No!" The Hawk struggled to his feet. He had to see her. He had to know everything that had happened to her.

With Derrick clinging to his arm, Hawk moved to the back of the ambulance. Mariner stepped in front of them. "Maybe you should wait."

"He's got to see her," Derrick said calmly.

Mariner could see that to try to stop him was futile. It was his wife. What right did he have to deny him? They gathered at the tailgate of the ambulance where the two paramedics guarded the remains. Mariner still hesitated.

"Show me!" The Hawk suddenly shouted. He was The Hawk with full, ferocious power.

Mariner stood beside them and slowly pulled the blanket back, beginning at the feet and then the torso. He hesitated. The Hawk was frozen as he watched. Mariner had no choice. He pulled back the blanket to reveal the full, ghastly truth.

Hawk stared at the remains of his lovely wife. The only person he had ever fully loved, reduced to this. Then it was even too much for him, and he burst into tears, sobbing as his friend Derrick held him.

Mariner covered the body and then had to turn away. Tears were flowing down his face. He thought of his daughter and all the women he had ever known. The horror—it was more than he could bear.

Alex was there for him and put his hand on his partner's shoulder for reassurance. "I've got to get that fucker," was all Mariner could say, but it was whispered so low that no one heard him.

Alex took over to give time for Mariner to collect himself. He took down the phone numbers of Derrick and The Hawk and explained where Shelly's body would be taken. The order was given, and the paramedics left, the lights flashing.

By then a television crew had arrived. The cameraman shot the scene, while the reporter went around talking to those who had witnessed the accident. The local municipal councillor had arrived and waited patiently. Once the camera was set up, the reporter began the interview with the politician.

"Councillor, this is another tragic traffic death of a cyclist. Do you have a comment?"

"I can tell you it is shocking. This is the second death of a cyclist in my ward alone since the beginning of the year. This just has to stop."

"The mayor has described the controversy between cyclists and drivers as a war against the car. Is that how you see it?"

"If there is a war, the casualties are cyclists, not drivers. We have to find ways to build our roads and streets so they are safer for everyone."

Mariner stopped listening to the interview. Derrick was taking The Hawk back home, where they would make the dreaded phone calls to relatives and friends. The crowd listened to the interview with the councillor. Once it was over, they began drifting away. Partners would be waiting; supper would be on the table; it was time to resume life.

Mariner and Alex talked to the other two witnesses. Their stories agreed with Metcalfe's. An argument broke out between the driver and a bike courier. The driver took the corner too fast, and the woman on the bike hit the side of the vehicle and fell under the back wheel. The only difference was that the second of the witnesses said that he was certain the SUV did not signal his turn.

After the interviews, the street was almost deserted. Mariner told the young uniformed policeman to call a tow truck to take the SUV to the pound. Then they got in their cruiser, with Abbott in the backseat, and drove away from the scene. The intersection of College and Dovercourt would soon be back to normal.

CHAPTER 5

Abbott, the driver of the SUV, sat in the backseat of the police car watching the action on the street with the police cars, the ambulance and the crowd milling about.

All I did was make a right turn, he told himself. *She should have seen me. Jesus, I mean, roads are for cars, not bikes. It wasn't my fuckin' fault that she was killed.*

The longer he sat alone, the more he convinced himself that he had done nothing wrong. The woman on the bicycle should have watched out for him.

Fuckin' cops. They're the problem. They want to get someone like me with a big car. Someone successful. That's it. They want to stick it to us—take the side of all the loafers and welfare recipients who hang out around here.

Abbott had been sitting in the car, stewing over this for a couple of minutes, before he remembered that he had his mobile phone in his pocket. He selected the number from the memory and held the phone up to his ear. It rang. "Come on! Pick up, Ricky." It was a Friday evening. Maybe they would ignore it. The phone rang six times before his brother answered.

"Hello."

"Ricky, it's me."

"Yeah?"

"Jesus, you know what? I'm in the backseat of a fuckin' police car."

"What?"

"Yeah." For a moment he felt panic. Maybe this time his brother wouldn't help him. "I was in an accident. That's all. Nothin' serious."

There was silence at the other end. "Why have they got you in a police car?"

"This woman.... Like, I was making a right-hand turn, and this fuckin' woman on a bicycle, she slammed into the side of my car."

"Was the car damaged?"

"Yeah. It's got a dent in it."

"Goddammit, Charlie. That's a leased car. You know it's going to push up our insurance rates."

"But it wasn't my fault, Ricky. I mean, all I did was make a fuckin' right-hand turn!"

"Were you drinking?"

"No. Well, I had one drink. The cops did a breathalyzer on me, but I couldn't have been over the limit."

"Well, then get out of there and go home. For Christ's sake, you can't afford to lose your licence." Ricky's voice showed his frustration with his brother.

"That's why I'm phonin' you. Like, I'm not sure what they're going to do."

"Who?"

"The police."

"Jesus, it's just a fender-bender."

"I killed a girl."

"What?"

"Yeah, like, it wasn't my fault."

"You *killed* a girl?"

"Like, all I did was make a right-hand turn, and she hit the side of the car and fell." Charlie was sweating now.

"And she's dead?" Ricky shouted.

"She fell under the car, and I rode over her."

"Jesus Christ! You're in deep shit now. What are you going to do?"

"I dunno. Like, that's why I'm phonin' you."

"Shit, Charlie, I can't bail you out all the time!"

The sweat beads were rolling down Charlie's chest now, and he didn't know what to say. He felt the panic deep in his stomach. Ricky had to help him. He always helped him.

"Tell me the whole thing."

"I did, Ricky. Jesus, you've got to believe me."

"Where were you?"

"Like, I was comin' along College Street, and, you know, there are these fuckin' people on bicycles everywhere. Thick with them, for Christ's sake, and the cars were lined up waiting for a red light. It was Dovercourt, I think. And I got up to the corner, and I turned right and then slam."

"Did you have your indicator light on?"

"Yeah, I think so. Sure, I must have."

"You'd better get that one straight."

"Sure, yeah. I put the blinker on for sure."

"Then what happened?"

"I just made the turn, and I heard her slam into the side of my car. She must have fallen because I felt the back wheel bump."

"Jesus." Ricky was silent, trying to think what to do.

"Then this cop came, and then there were these people on the street yelling at me. It was a zoo down here."

"I bet."

"I talked to this one detective."

"Did you say anything to him?"

"All I said was that it wasn't my fault."

"Nothing more?"

"No."

"Good. Don't tell him anything else."

"But they've got me sitting in the backseat of this cop car. I don't know what they're going to do with me."

"Okay, okay." An action plan had fallen into place for Ricky. "Just stay there, okay? Do what the cops want you to do, but don't tell them anything, okay? I'm going to get you some help. I'll phone you back." Then he hung up quickly. He didn't want to hear any more from Charlie.

Ricky's wife, Leona, was leaning up against the kitchen counter listening to his side of the conversation. The call had come during their dinner, and their meal was getting cold on the table. She already knew there was trouble.

"What's he done now?" she asked.

Ricky was looking up the phone number in the memory of his mobile. "He's been in an accident and killed somebody."

"Oh, no! Was he drinking?"

"He says not, but you know. He almost lost his licence that other time."

"Maybe they'll get him this time. Are you still going to help him?"

"He's my brother, for God's sake."

"He's nothing but trouble, if you ask me."

But the phone on the other end of the line was ringing. Ricky turned away from his wife so he could concentrate. He didn't like phoning on a Friday night, but he knew that Bert would be home and this was an emergency. It rang four times before a woman answered. She put Bert on the phone.

"You're not going to like this, Bert."

"What is it?"

"You remember my brother, Charlie?"

"Yeah."

"He's been in a driving accident in the city. Says he's killed someone."

"Where is he now?" Bert was always calm. That's why Ricky liked him and had come to rely on him. He was the company's corporate lawyer.

"In a police car down on College Street."

"What do you want me to do?" Bert was a partner in one of the big Bay Street law firms. Charlie's company paid him a retainer every month. That guaranteed service.

"Somebody's got to get down there and help him. God knows what he'd say if he faced those cops alone."

"You know that criminal law is not my field, but I think I can get someone from the firm to act on his behalf if you guarantee the fee."

Charlie already felt a sense of relief. "That'd be good."

"I know this young lawyer. He's really smart."

"Get him if you can."

"Who's the client, your brother or the company?"

"My brother, but the company will guarantee the fee."

"Okay. I'll have him phone you, and you can give him the details."

"Fine." And Ricky hung up.

He stood by the phone for a long moment, trying to think it through. What else could he do? Charlie was his brother. He'd promised their mom that he would look after him. This wasn't the first jackpot he'd been in. Ricky even hired him to be a salesman because he couldn't stand the thought of Charlie unemployed and his family on welfare. He wasn't much of a salesman, but it didn't really matter. The refrigeration units sold themselves. His wife said that Charlie wasn't his responsibility, but blood is thicker than water. What else could he do?

Ricky and Leona had sat down at the dining-room table to finish dinner when the phone rang.

"Mr. Abbott?"

"Yes?"

"This is James Underhill. Bert asked me to call."

"Thank you. I'm sorry to bother you on a Friday night, but my brother is in trouble."

"So I understand."

Ricky gave Underhill the details of his brother's name and mobile phone number and hung up.

CHAPTER 6

Charlie Abbott got the phone call from the lawyer as the police car was making its way to the station. He started to explain the circumstances when the lawyer interrupted him

"I'll get those details later. Tell me where you are going so we can meet."

"Just a moment." Charlie leaned forward. "Where are you taking me?" he asked the detective.

"Fifty-two Division, 255 Dundas Street West."

"Fine," the lawyer said in his precise way. "I will meet you there in a few minutes. In the meantime, I don't want you to talk to the police or make a statement or anything. Just wait until I get there, and we will discuss it."

"Okay," Charlie said and hung up. He felt a real sense of relief. He knew Ricky would deliver. His brother always knew what to do.

James Underhill, the lawyer, calmly finished his dinner. There was no hurry. The police would keep his client on ice until he got there.

"Do you really have to go out?" his girlfriend asked.

"Someone is in trouble, and they've turned to me." Rita was a lovely woman, but she really didn't understand the world of lawyers. "It's not far. The police station is just over on Dundas, near the art gallery. I won't be too long."

"Too bad," and she looked at him in her coy way.

"You go ahead with the movie. I'll get back as soon as I can."

"I'll miss you," and she smiled.

They had planned a quiet evening at home in his condo. Dinner, a movie and then, well, it was certain there would be nice things after that. He had been working so hard lately—60-, 70-hour weeks—that he didn't have much time to spend with her. He was a litigator, and preparing an important civil suit for one of the firm's major corporate clients. If he could make a success of this case, it would help to create his reputation, and that was absolutely essential if he was to become one of the top litigators in the country. It took talent and hard work. He was confident that he had plenty of the first, and he knew he had to put in the preparation time. He would make it happen.

Still, he liked criminal cases. They were simpler, and they involved real people with flesh and blood and guts. Corporate law all hung on things like the interpretations of contracts and other legal agreements. Criminal law could be flamboyant. If all else failed, there was the possibility of an impassioned plea to a judge or jury about the good name of the client. He especially liked the sound of this case. It was a guarantee of a good feand all expenses paid. That didn't come in criminal law very often, and he intended to take advantage of it.

James finished his dinner and got ready. For a moment he was going to put on a tie but then rejected it. This was a Friday night, after all, and no one would expect even a lawyer to wear a tie to go to one of Toronto's divisional police headquarters. He gave Rita a peck on the cheek, just like a middle-aged husband, and then was out the door with a cheerful wave.

He caught a taxi over to the station. It wasn't far, but why walk or take the car? The client was paying the ticket. The police station was an ugly, modern building—something that police officers would think was sophisticated. Its best feature was the glass bricks on the outside walls, but once inside, the building was like all of the other cop shops in the city: plain white walls broken only with photos of police officers usually standing beside their cars. Over the head of the duty sergeant, posted close to the front door, was the Toronto police crest with their motto: "To Serve and Protect."

He announced himself to the sergeant. "I am James Underhill, the lawyer for Mr. Charles Abbott. I understand that Mr. Abbott was brought to this station because of some driving incident." He spoke precisely and clearly. That was his style, but he knew this impressed policemen.

The sergeant nodded. "Detective Mariner is handling the case."

"I would like to speak to my client, please."

"Take a seat."

"I'm sorry. This is important. It is alleged that my client is facing serious charges. I must see him now." Polite but firm was how to get attention. If you don't demand respect, the police will walk all over you. That was not going to happen to James Underhill.

"It is going to take a moment, sir. They are just booking him."

"What is the charge?"

"You will have to talk to Detective Mariner about that."

"I have the right to full access to my client." He stood stiff and erect, projecting the authority of an advocate.

The duty sergeant considered the young lawyer a moment and then picked up the phone and dialled the number. "This is front desk. Get me Mariner," he ordered.

He held onto the line for what seemed to be a long time while the young lawyer paced back and forth. Other people in the waiting room watched passively. Finally, Mariner came on the line.

"There's a young lawyer by the name of Underhill out in the front here demanding to speak to his client, the one you are charging with a driving offence."

"Let him wait."

"He's one of those blue-blood types demanding service," the duty sergeant whispered.

"We're just charging this guy. I'll be out in a minute."

It was more like five minutes before Detective Mariner came into the waiting room. Underhill was still pacing. They exchanged names and shook hands.

"What's the charge?" the lawyer asked. He kept his voice low so others in the waiting room could not hear.

"We charged him with second-degree murder."

"Second-degree murder?" Underhill was alarmed. "That's an extremely serious charge. This was just a driving accident."

"A woman was killed, Mr. Underhill. The charges might be even more serious once the Crown looks at it."

"You can't do that!" Only premeditated murder was more serious than second-degree murder.

"There is evidence that the accused intended to kill the victim. As I said, the Crown will review it, but at the moment the second-degree murder charge stays." Mariner was firm.

"You sound angry." The lawyer slipped that in as if it were a casual comment, but he was looking for any sign of prejudice against his client.

"Someone was killed. That is serious." Mariner knew not to fall into lawyers' traps.

"Can I talk to my client?"

"We will begin our questioning of him in a few minutes."

"Will he be allowed bail?"

"You can ask, but bail is never allowed in a serious charge like this without the approval of a judge."

"It is very unusual to have a second-degree murder charge for a traffic accident."

"This is not a normal traffic accident."

They eyed each other uneasily. "Do you want to see your client?" Mariner asked.

"Of course."

Mariner abruptly turned and walked toward the door he had come out of. He swiped the electronic pad with his plastic key and opened the door. Underhill followed. They walked to the holding cells at the back of the building.

Mariner spoke to the officer in charge. "This is James Underhill, the lawyer for Abbott, who we brought in earlier. Let him speak to his client. We will begin our interrogation in a few minutes."

"I assume I will be allowed to sit in on the interrogation?" The lawyer was more cautious now.

"Of course. That's your right." Already Mariner did not like Underhill's sense of superiority. "Five minutes, then we start the interrogation," the detective added

Underhill was starting to have an intense dislike for this brusque, self-assured detective. The guard brought Charles Abbott into Interrogation Room One. They shook hands as they exchanged names and settled into the hard metal chairs covered with black vinyl.

"So tell me what happened?" the lawyer began.

"It's all bullshit, you know. I'm so fuckin' mad. They put me in a goddamn cell like I was some fuckin' criminal."

"Just tell me what happened."

"I was driving down College Street and…."

"East or west?"

"I was headin' west. Like, I was just minding my business, and the street was crawling with those fuckin' bicycles. You wouldn't believe how many there were on the street. And so I drove along, just lookin' around, you know, and then I made a right turn on Dovercourt and this cyclist, she slammed into the side of my car." Abbott paused for a moment.

"And then what happened?"

"She must have fallen or somethin' 'cause I rode over her."

"Is she dead?"

"Yeah. But it wasn't my fault. Why wasn't she looking where she was going?"

"So that's all?"

"Yeah. It was an accident."

"Okay. Seems simple enough." Underhill smiled to reassure his client. "Then why did they charge you with second-degree murder?"

"I dunno. Christ. What's that mean, anyhow? Second-degree murder? I didn't shoot anybody."

Only Underhill did not have time to answer. There was a knock on the door, it opened and the two plain-clothes detectives entered. Alex was introduced to Underhill, and the two sides settled into chairs on either side of the table. Alex took out his pad and pen while Mariner did all of the talking for their side.

First he named all of the people in the room and repeated the charges against the accused. Then he continued.

"This interrogation is being video recorded. I warn you that the recording may be entered in evidence in case of a trial. Anything that you say may be used against you. Do you understand?"

Abbott nodded.

"Describe to us what happened leading up to the accident and the death of Shelly McTavish."

Abbott repeated the story in the same detail as he had told the lawyer. "I was going west on College Street, turned right on Dovercourt and felt a thump on the side of my car. That's all I know."

"How fast were you travelling?"

"I don't know. Like, not fast. The cars were backed up at the Dovercourt light. I couldn't have been going fast."

"How fast were you going as you went around the corner?"

"Not fast. I mean, I was stopped for the light, and as the cars ahead of me went through, I turned right."

"Quickly?"

"No."

"We have witnesses who say you turned very abruptly. You speeded up as you went around the corner. Is that right?"

"What do they know? They weren't there."

"These were witnesses of the accident."

Underhill put his hand on Abbott's arm. "He says there was nothing out of the ordinary in the way he took the corner."

"Mr. Underhill, do not answer for your client. It is his explanation that we want, not yours."

The lawyer glared at Mariner. Who was this policeman to tell him how to defend his client?

"Mr. Abbott, did you signal your turn onto Dovercourt?"

"Yeah, sure I did. I always signal turns."

"Are you certain?"

"Yeah."

"We have a witness who says you did not signal your turn. Do you want to revise or change your statement?"

Abbott looked at his lawyer, but Underhill felt he could not prompt him. "No, I'm telling the truth, for Christ's sake. I put on my signal like I always do."

"Did you see Shelly McTavish in the bicycle lane as you made your turn?"

"What?" He felt a sudden surge of panic. He was trying to trick him.

"Did you see Ms. McTavish in the bike lane as you made your turn?"

"Yeah. Of course I did."

"Then why didn't you stop?"

"Stop? I did stop right after she thumped the side of my car."

"That's not the question. Did you see her before you made your turn?"

"Yes."

"Then you would know that she was very close and she was travelling fast on her bicycle. Why didn't you stop before you crossed the bike lane in front of her?"

Abbott looked at his lawyer desperate to find the right answer, but he was no help. "I mean, I don't know. It was an accident. That's all I know."

Mariner pressed the point. "What are you telling us? Did you see her or not?"

"I dunno, for fuck sake. It happened so fast."

"At first you said you saw her and now you say you didn't see her. What is the truth?" Mariner demanded sharply.

"He answered your question," Underhill said. "He doesn't know."

"Mr. Underhill, if you answer for your client one more time, you will leave this room! You're here to interpret the law for your client, not bend the story!"

"Who are you to tell me?"

"I am the chief investigating officer of this case, and I have every right to ask these questions! We are trying to determine the truth! A young woman has been killed!—killed, Mr. Underhill!" Mariner was shouting now, but he was in control. Watching. Testing. "If you interrupt me one more time you are out of here. Understand?"

Underhill was unnerved. Nothing in his legal training or practice prepared him for this.

Mariner turned back to the accused and continued. "Mr. Abbott, were you driving erratically as you were driving west on College Street before the accident?"

Abbott was panicked now. "No. It was just normal, like. There was nothin'."

"Are you certain?"

"Fuckin' right!" Who was he to doubt his word?

"Did you drive into the bike lane?"

"No!"

"Are you certain of that?"

"Yeah. God's truth. Never."

"Were you upset about something?"

"No."

"Did you get angry at anyone?"

"No. Like I was just drivin' along. What are you askin' that for?"

"Just answer the question."

"I was driving normally."

"We have witnesses who say you got into a shouting match with a bike courier a short time before Ms. McTavish was killed because your car kept coming into the bicycle lane."

"That's not true. I never went into the fuckin' bike lane." Now Abbott was shouting.

"Did you get into an angry exchange with a bike courier?"

"Oh, that kid. What the fuck does he know?"

"Did you shout at him?"

"Look, he was nothin'. I mean, yeah, we had words back and forth. But it was nothin', you know."

"That's not what we have been told."

"Then they're fuckin' lying!"

"I guess you never get angry, Mr. Abbott."

"What is all this bullshit? I mean, it was a fuckin' accident. Like, Christ, I've got a good job. My brother's Richard Abbott, you…you must know him. He's got a big factory and everything. Why are you picking on me?"

Mariner got to his feet. He had had enough. "We are not picking on you," he said slowly. "A woman has been killed, and we are trying to get at the truth. You aren't helping." He looked at the young lawyer, who seemed equally panicked by the onslaught of words.

"Mr. Abbott, you have been charged with second-degree murder. On Monday morning a Crown attorney will review the charges and the evidence that we have collected. A decision will be made at that time as to what charges the Crown will proceed with."

By that time, Underhill, had collected himself. "What are the chances that Mr. Abbott can get bail tonight?"

"You have the right to request bail from the justice of the peace, but it is very rare that bail is granted on a charge this serious without it being reviewed by a provincial court judge.

"You mean I've got to stay in this place?" Abbott demanded.

"That is up to the justice of the peace." Mariner opened the door and held it until Alex could join him, and then they closed it behind them.

As they were going into the detective's room, Alex touched Mariner's arm and they stopped. "You'll never get it to stick," he whispered so others would not hear.

"What?"

"The second-degree murder charge—the Crown will never go for it." Alex had never seen his partner upset like this.

"Maybe not."

"Dangerous driving, but nothing more than that."

"We'll see."

"It's your reputation. They'll think you've gone nuts."

"If I worried about my reputation, Alex, I couldn't sleep at night."

After the policemen had left, Abbott turned to his lawyer. "Do I have to stay in this fuckin' hole all weekend? I'm gonna go fuckin' crazy in here. Like, Monday, and even then they might not let me out."

The lawyer was already wondering what he would tell Bert. He was a senior partner of his law firm, and the corporate lawyer of Richard Abbott's company. This would be a colossal failure in his eyes. But there was nothing he could do.

Underhill waited for the justice of the peace. He had to be able to tell Bert that he had done everything possible to get his client released on bail.

The police were busy bringing in the drunks and junkies who got out of hand in the bars and Friday night parties. The lawyer sat on a hard wooden bench listening to the wails and cries, trying to understand what it all meant, but his background and fine training made that impossible.

Finally, at about 2:30 in the morning, the justice of the peace appeared. Abbott was brought out of his cell, and the J.P. listened to the lawyer's appeal for bail, but he wouldn't consider it. A second-degree murder charge was far too serious for him to deal with. A judge would review the charges on Monday and make the decision about bail, he explained.

When James Underhill finally got back to his fashionable condo and climbed into bed beside Rita, his brash self-confidence was deeply shaken.

Alex headed home at midnight, the end of their shift. He was a family man, and tomorrow there would be hockey with the boys and shopping with his wife. Mariner stayed behind to write the report on Abbott and the accident. There was no one at home for him. He felt better working on the report in the station rather than facing the lonely apartment.

The Saturday newspapers would be filled with the news that a young woman had been killed riding her bicycle. The politicians and commentators would be all over this one. The chief and the Crown would demand to see his report. Mariner wanted it to be good.

CHAPTER 7

The weekend newspapers, radio, TV stations and postings online focused on the death of a young mother and cyclist in an accident, and the war between drivers and cyclists.

One newspaper account described the accident, and then went on to give a description of Shelly McTavish, crushed under the wheels of the big SUV. The article was illustrated with a photo of the young mother holding her baby, both smiling radiantly.

> "Shelly was born and raised in Mississauga and came to live in downtown Toronto to attend the Ontario College of Art and Design. Her parents, Herbert and Marilyn McTavish, describe her as a happy, optimistic person who excelled in athletics and was an accomplished artist. A teacher at OCAD said she was a very promising costume designer.
>
> She married the avant-garde artist Samuel Dockstader, who signs his work "The Hawk." Shelly was devoted to her 14-month-old baby, Marilyn.

They lived in the west end of the city, with every reason to expect a happy and prosperous future. That future has now been crushed.

And an account from another newspaper.

Already a memorial for Shelly has blossomed on the northeast corner of College and Dovercourt. Flowers lean up against a lamppost mere yards away from the fatal spot where she died. Cards and hand-painted signs are arranged between the blossoms. One sign reads: "You will not be forgotten in the struggle for cycle city."

A group of cyclists arrives, wheeling a painted white bicycle, which they chain and lock to a telephone pole at the intersection. This is a "ghost bike," marking the spot where yet another cyclist has died in the city.

Already Shelly McTavish has become a symbol in the battle between "car culture" and "bike culture," the ongoing guerrilla warfare that is intensifying in our city."

One of the television stations repeated a news clip of an interview with a downtown city councillor.

"I think the mayor of Toronto has contributed to this problem by saying things like roads are for cars and trucks, not bicycles. He even went so far as to say when cyclists are killed it's their own fault. I think this has contributed to the more aggressive behaviour of drivers that we are seeing. The mayor should be working toward a safer city, not contributing to the conflict."

A suburban city councillor leapt to the mayor's defence:

"We are all shocked and saddened by the death of a young mother, but cyclists in the city constantly flout the Highway Safety Act. The mayor believes, like I do, that it is time that cyclists begin to behave in a more responsible way by following the rules."

And the people carried the debate to the blogs and online newspaper columns with their own heated comments.

"Why do cyclists have to compete with cars and trucks for a little bit of road space? Only cyclists suffer when they come into conflict with cars."

"I was driving down a one-way street listening to a news account of the tragic death of Shelly McTavish when suddenly a cyclist was coming straight at me. It was dark. The cyclist didn't have a light or a reflector, he wasn't wearing a helmet and he was coming the wrong way down a one-way street. I could have hit him. Cyclists have to follow the traffic rules."

"What we need is separated bike lanes protected by a concrete barrier, not just lines painted on the street. Anyone cycling along College knows that simply marking the road with paint just does not work."

"Driving in Toronto is crazy. The drivers talk on their cell phones as they rush to get to where they are going. They race to make a turn and then have to jam on their brakes to stop before they hit a pedestrian or a cyclist. It's a wonder there aren't more killings."

"The problem is that cyclists get no respect and so they act like a bunch of anarchists. They flout the traffic rules and give drivers the finger and get into shouting matches. When the drivers give cyclists respect, then maybe cyclists will start obeying the rules."

"Cyclists pay property taxes. Why don't they get the same protection as drivers?"

"Drivers pay for the roads with gasoline taxes. When cyclists start paying road taxes, then they can have a share of the road."

"I am angry because I bike to work every day, and I have had far too many close calls with cars. But most of all I'm angry because I don't see any possibility of change. There is no political leadership, just two sides shouting at each other."

"Cyclists should be licensed and insured, just like car drivers. When they break the rules, their licence should be taken away from them."

"Cycling is a great way to get around and healthy, too. We need to redesign our roads to provide protected barriers for cyclists. That will make our roads safer for everyone."

"I'm a cyclist in the downtown core, and in the last 10 years it has become a lot more dangerous. There are more condos, more people, more cars and more bicycles. Something has to be done or there will be a lot more people killed, just like Shelly McTavish."

CHAPTER 8

Spider Smith was watching the TV news on Saturday night with his girlfriend, Jay, when the clip on Shelly's death was repeated. He was so shocked that he jumped to his feet and ran his fingers through his long hair.

"Christ, do you see that?"

"What?" Jay asked.

"When did that happen?" He pointed at the TV set.

"Friday night, I think. That's been playing all day."

"I think I was there. Holy Christ. College and Davenport. Yeah, I'm sure of it."

"When?"

"Friday night, around seven. I was making one last delivery, and I was comin' along College, and I saw him."

"Saw who?"

"The guy in that there car." But the image on the TV screen had changed, and they were playing an ad. "Turn the fuckin' thing off."

Jay worked the remote, and the TV went dead. "What are you saying?" She was concerned. Every time Spider got wired, it was very hard to cool him down.

"The car that they were showing on the TV, the SUV that killed the girl, I got into an argument with the guy driving that car."

"Are you sure?"

"It's got to be. It was a big SUV. He was all over the fuckin' road. Comin' into the bike lane and everything. Almost hit me, the bastard. Those fuckin' bike lanes are useless. I got into a shouting match with him."

"With the driver?"

"Yeah, I'm sure of it. I shouted at him to stay out of the bike lane. I was really pissed. I mean, he was all over the fuckin' place, swerving around. I could see him. He came into the bike lane more than once. Son of a bitch. He must have gone on and killed the girl right after that." Spider was very agitated now.

"How do you know that?"

"The accident was on the corner of College and Davenport. That's what they said on the TV. That prick! I should have done him right there!"

"Come on, Spider. You're supposed to keep calm."

"Jesus, Jay. If she was killed...!"

"She was killed all right."

"Maybe I had somethin' to do with it."

"You weren't even there!"

"But I got into a shouting match with this son of a bitch." Spider put his hands through his long hair again. He felt panic. He paced back and forth.

"Calm down. What happened?"

"I shouted at him."

"Tell me carefully." She knew she had to bring him down if she was to get the full story.

Spider breathed deeply. That was the technique he had been taught to help him gain control.

"Sit down and tell me from the beginning so I can understand."

Spider sat on the chesterfield beside her. Other than the TV, it was the only furniture in the bare room. Jay put her hand on his arm to help calm him. He was difficult. In the past he had been in a lot of trouble, but she knew deep down he was a good man.

"I had to make this delivery in the west end, there, and I went along College 'cause it's the only bike path heading west. And as I was ridin' along there west of Bathurst, I noticed this SUV, a big, dark car, Jesus, bigger than any of the other cars on the street, and he was comin' into the bike lane. Like, three times at least I saw him do it. Once he almost forced this guy off his bike. So I got.... Well, you know me. I got upset. And so this guy in the SUV stopped at the light, and so I shouted at him."

"What did you say?"

"Keep in your own lane. Somethin' like that."

"Did he say anything back to you?"

"He was rolling down his window to say somethin', but I took off on my bike."

"If that's all that happened, then...."

"But then he caught up with me. He raced after me, and then turned his car into the bike lane. Almost hit me. I mean, I almost lost it right there, Jay. I mean, I could have been hurt, so I freaked out."

"You know, Spider, you've got to be careful in times like that. Isn't that what the therapist says?"

He put his head in his hands. Even talking about it was hard.

"But he almost hit me, Jay. I mean, shit! So I tried to be cool. I put my bike up against a parking meter or tree or somethin' and I went around to the driver's side, and I was gonna have it out with him."

"Oh, Spider, you've got to be careful. You can't get into another fight. You know they said the next time…."

"No, I was cool. I really was, Jay. You've gotta believe me. I mean, I didn't even swear or nothin' like that. I just told him to stay out of the bike lane. That's all, but he got panicked, and he floored his fuckin' car, and it spun out of control and up over the sidewalk, and then back onto the road. Jesus, what an asshole!"

"Then what did you do?"

"I knew I had to get out of there before the cops came or something like that. So I got on my bike and crossed the street, and I went up to the corner and then went south on Dovercourt. I made the delivery and came home."

"Are you sure?"

"Yes!"

"Then you don't know anything about the accident?"

"It must have happened right after I left. She was hit right at the corner. That's what they said on the TV. The guy must have made a right turn from College onto Dovercourt, and he killed her right there. I didn't see it."

"Then you didn't have anything to do with it."

Spider sat on the edge of the chesterfield, running through every detail in his mind. He combed his hair with his fingers like he always did when he was upset. Every detail was as vivid as if it were happening right before him. When he turned and looked at Jay, he felt very calm.

"What must have happened is that he didn't see me cross the street behind his car. He thought I would be still coming up the right-hand lane behind him. He saw the girl in the side mirror of his car, and he thought it was me. He got up to the corner, and she was just behind him, and he did a sharp right-hand turn. He was trying to get me, but he killed the girl instead."

"No, Spider. It can't be."

He reviewed it all in his mind again. The shouting match, the fear in the face of the driver, the SUV spinning out of control, the car stopped behind the line of cars waiting at the light, he disappears, and the girl takes his place riding up to the stoplight. The SUV turns, and she falls and is crushed under the back wheel.

"That's what happened. He was trying to kill me, and he killed the girl by mistake."

"Oh, God!"

They sat in silence for a moment. "What should I do?" he asked.

"But you didn't cause the accident, Spider."

"Maybe I did. I got the guy angry. You know what happens when I get angry. Maybe he's the same."

"But he's got to control his anger. Isn't that what your therapist says to you? It's okay to get angry, but you can't lose control and hurt others. Isn't that what she says?"

"Yeah, but...."

"He couldn't control his anger. It's not your fault, Spider. It's his fault."

He was nodding because she was right.

"You didn't get into a fight with him, did you? You just left, but he couldn't control himself, and he killed the girl."

"Yeah, that must be what happened." He was beginning to feel better.

"But what are you going to do now?" Jay asked.

"What do you mean?"

"Like, are you going to go to the police?"

"The cops?"

"Don't you think you should?"

"Tell them what?"

"Just tell them what happened. They said on the news that the police are doing an investigation."

"I don't go near the cops."

"But the girl was killed."

"I don't trust the cops after what happened to me."

He got to his feet and began to pace. "You don't understand the cops. They take one look at me and that's it. They'll find something that I did wrong. I want nothin' to do with cops. Understand?"

She could see how agitated he had become. "All right. Okay. You did nothing wrong. That's the important thing."

He was staring at her. "Why do you think I should go to the cops?"

"What if it was me? Dead. Out there lying on the street with this big car that had run me over. Would you go to the cops for me? Would you tell them what happened? Would you do it for me?"

"I'd get the fucker who did it."

"A lot of good that would do. Me, dead, lying there in the street, and the cops looking for witnesses. Would you talk to them then?"

"But you don't understand!"

"Yes, I do."

"You think I'm a shithead for not wanting to go to the cops. You know what they'd do? The assholes! They'd take one look at me, and they'd call me up on their fuckin' computer, and they'd see my record. Two years less a day for dealin' dope. Then there's that assault charge. You know how lucky I was to get out of that charge? I had to promise to go to the fuckin' therapist and then probation. If it wasn't for you and having my job as a courier I'd have been back in the slammer or Kingston or Christ knows. I don't want to go near that shit anymore. You understand?" He was shouting now. "You understand?"

"Yes, Spider, I understand. Okay. I'll drop it."

She watched him pace back and forth, back and forth.

"They can really fuck up your head, you know. Like, it's them or us. When you're in the slammer, you've got nothing and no way to get at them. The fuckin' guards are out to get you, and three-quarters of the guys inside are the same—worse even. They're happy to see you go down 'cause it means that you're lower than them. I had to pull myself back up from that shit, Jay. That was fuckin' hard. You don't know how hard."

"It's over now, Spider."

"No, it's not. It's never over. They're still out there waiting for me to fuck up so they can send me back. That would make them happy. When I was gettin' out, one of the guards told me, 'We'll see you here again. Guys like you keep us in business.' Yeah, he said that to me, the fucker."

"But you proved them wrong."

"Look, there's only one thing I've learned, and that is to stay as far away from the cops as possible because they're just lookin' for a chance to send guys like me back."

He paced again. Then he slowed. Deep breath, deep breath, he told himself and he sucked the air deep into his lungs. That's what the therapist told him, and it helped. Jay was sitting on the edge of the chesterfield, watching his every move. God, she was the only one who had stuck with him. What would he do if she left him?

"You still think I should go to the cops about the accident?" he said.

"Spider, I think you have to do what you think is right."

He sat down beside her, and Jay put her arms around his shoulders and held him. She could feel his physical power, but deep inside he was like a frightened, abandoned little boy. She knew he had so much to be frightened about. His mother left him. He had lived on the street. Jail. Fights. Booze. Hard drugs. She had been through some of the same. It was one day at a time. Control the anger. Keep off the booze and the drugs. Work every day. Try to stay clean. They didn't need this crap about the accident.

He was quiet for a long time as she held him, and then finally he spoke. "Okay. I'll go down and see the cops."

"You sure, Spider?"

"Like you say, it could have been you or somebody else. The guy meant to kill me, but he killed the girl by mistake."

"Yeah."

"The cops should know that. Right?"

"Yeah."

He was quiet again, and she still held him. "Will you come with me?" he asked quietly.

"Course I will."

"Thanks, 'cause they scare the piss out of me. That's the truth." And he smiled for the first time in a long time.

CHAPTER 9

Sarah Simonac, the Crown attorney, waited for Detective Mariner. The documents describing the charges against Charles Abbott lay on her desk, with the phrase "second-degree murder" in clear type. This gave an unusual twist to what seemed like a straightforward dangerous driving causing bodily harm case. She had read through his report and watched the video of the interrogation. She had even seen the news report on Citytv and read the *Toronto Star*'s account. She needed to talk to the detective to sort out the facts so she could figure out what to do next.

This case was already getting out of hand. The news stories on the weekend had stirred up the public. A lawyer by the name of James Underhill had left messages on her voicemail before nine o'clock in the morning. He was "outraged" that his client had been held in jail with no opportunity for bail over the weekend. She knew all of the defence lawyers in the city, but she had never heard of Underhill. What caught her attention was that he was from the big Bay Street law firm of Munro, Stafford and

Malone. Not many of the accused going through the lower court in the Old City Hall could afford pricy council like that.

This was big news in the city. The mayor had begun his term by denouncing the "war against the car." That had stirred up the cyclists and community activists. Now a young, attractive woman—a mother with a baby just over a year old—had been killed on a city street riding in a bicycle lane. One of the councillors had even gone as far as to say that there was a war against cyclists because the city refused to build barriers along the bike paths to protect them.

She knew that she was going to get caught between an enraged public, the politicians, the media, a top Bay Street defence lawyer using every trick in the book to get his client off, and her obligation to ensure that there was a fair trial. The second-degree murder charge at least had made the public think that the authorities were taking the killing seriously, but it would make the case that much more complicated to handle.

Today she would have to make a statement to the press on behalf of the Crown. After that, all she could do was sit back and watch while the media mangled and distorted the details. As far as the public was concerned, the only thing that was important was that a young woman, full of promise, had been killed, and they wanted justice—revenge. How could anything as clumsy as the law or the system of courts bring justice in a case like this?

It would be very important to communicate to the public that the courts were treating the case with the utmost seriousness, but still leave the impression that the accused would only be convicted once all of the facts have been considered by the judge. It was a delicate dance, and she had to get it right.

She knew that she was good at her job, but sometimes she felt beaten down by the role she had to play as Crown attorney. She was supposed to protect the public, but she didn't make the law. She wasn't the judge, and yet she was expected to voice the public's concerns for safety. She didn't have any magic answers for what happened out there on the streets, and yet people still looked to her to deliver justice.

Usually it didn't matter. No one was much interested in the pious statements of a Crown attorney, but she knew the press was looking for a way to keep a case like this alive. Every story would be accompanied by the photo that was in the *Star* that morning of a beautiful young woman with her baby, both of them with cheerful smiles. They looked like they had everything in the world. It was that photo that had grabbed the public's attention, and they would want to know why her death was allowed to happen.

A knock came to her office door and it was Detective Mariner. She had seen his face around the courts many times and read his name in the paper, but this was the first time she was able to connect the two. She didn't get to her feet when he came into the room. The detective leaned across the desk and shook her hand, and then they got straight to business.

"I've read your report and looked at the video," the Crown attorney said. "I take it you are the lead officer on the case?"

Mariner nodded.

"Were you the one who decided on the charge of second-degree murder?"

"Yes."

"Why didn't you settle on dangerous driving?"

"Because it was more than dangerous driving. Abbott was totally irresponsible. It should be second-degree murder at least, even murder."

"How could you justify murder?"

"He was driving in a completely reckless way. I believe he intended to cause her death."

The Crown stared at him for a moment. "I was told you had a reputation as a soft-headed liberal."

"Reputations are always misleading."

She nodded warily. He wasn't what she was expecting. Attractive, yes, slim, strong, but none of that simple boy's club manner that most of the policemen she met presented. Mariner seemed rigid, remote, but attentive to everything.

"You'll never get murder," she continued. "In order to prove that you would have to demonstrate that he set out purposely to kill this young woman. Premeditation. Can you prove that?"

"Abbott is without any feelings of guilt. He doesn't care that he killed someone or that he was erratic in his driving. He is only interested in saving his own skin."

"That's the way a lot of them are. That doesn't make them murderers."

"That's why I decided on the charge of second-degree murder."

"How do you justify that charge?" The Crown was sharp and tough. Mariner liked that.

"This accident could have been avoided, but through the gross negligence of Abbott, he killed the girl with his car. In the interrogation, first he said he said he saw the girl. Then he said he wasn't sure if he saw her. He is shopping around for the right answer."

"That doesn't justify a murder charge. His lawyer will say he's under stress and can't remember."

Mariner was not ready to give up. "If two people were playing with a loaded gun and it went off, killing one of them, you would not hesitate to charge the other with second-degree murder or manslaughter because his action demonstrated gross negligence causing death. That's what I'm saying happened in this case. It was the gross negligence of Abbott that caused her death, and that's second-degree murder."

She looked at him for a long moment. Mariner knew the law, and his argument was expressed in such a forceful, confident way that most would have been convinced, but she knew he was wrong.

"You will have a very tough time making a charge like that stick in a Toronto court. His defence lawyer will argue that it was an accident. Abbott lost his concentration for a moment. He didn't mean to do it. He's sorry and all of that stuff. The accused is given the benefit of the doubt in our courts, you will remember. Do you have any witnesses, detective, that will say that they saw him acting with gross negligence?"

"You read my report. We've got witnesses who say that he was driving all over the road. He went into the bike lane and almost hit a cyclist. He didn't signal his turn and went around the corner too fast. The girl didn't have a chance."

"You don't like the guy. I can see that, but none of this will get you a second-degree murder conviction."

"My feelings about him are irrelevant, but the feelings of the public are not irrelevant. They know a young, innocent woman was killed—a mother—and they already have decided it should not have happened. Let the judge figure out whether he is guilty of second-degree murder or not. That's what they get paid to do. Our job is to protect people like this woman."

"That's your job. I have to ensure the accused gets a fair trial. What if he is found not guilty and walks free? What will the public say?"

"Then maybe there would be such outrage that something would change."

"This system doesn't change. Only we change." She was thinking of herself as she made that statement. She had changed immeasurably since she had started this job.

"I won't support second-degree murder," she continued. "The charges in this case will be altered to dangerous driving causing bodily harm—Section 249 of the Criminal Code."

Mariner sat in silence. It was her decision. He had given it the best pitch he could and lost. Still, better to aim high then to give up before the struggle.

"Dangerous driving is a very strong charge," she added. "It is an indictable offence with up to 14 years' jail sentence, and he could have his licence taken away for a long time."

"They never give the maximum sentence."

"It's the best we can do. At least with the dangerous driving, you've got a chance to get a conviction. You will never get it with second-degree murder."

She shuffled through the papers on her desk for a moment. "Do you know where they're keeping Abbott? It's not in any of the papers."

"He's still over in the cells at 52 Division."

"I am going to do the paperwork to change the charge, and then there will be a bail hearing today."

"His lawyer, Underhill, is pretty worked up because the J.P. wouldn't give him bail on Friday night," added Mariner.

"I imagine he is. I've had two phone calls from him this morning."

"Let him squirm."

Sarah studied him for a moment. "You're pretty worked up about this case."

"You didn't see the girl lying on the street, or listen to the grief of the husband."

"If you talk like that on the witness stand the defence will make mincemeat of you."

"Think I haven't been through this before?"

She was all business again. "Get Abbott brought down here to Old City Hall. We will get new charges sworn out. Then there will be another bail hearing. We'll get one of the judges to do that, not a J.P. Then I have to talk to the press. They've been after me all morning."

"You too?"

"Have you talked to them?"

"Only to tell them the charges. I try to avoid the press as much as possible."

"It's part of my job, but I hate it. They can never get the facts straight."

Mariner was on his feet. "It will take me half an hour to get him here."

He was about to go out the door when she asked, "Are you going to oppose bail?"

"I have to."

"I wouldn't, but then that's your business."

"It's not all about winning and losing, you know. Sometimes you have to stand up for what is right."

She looked at him as he stood by the door. What was this detective up to anyway?

"Who's going to call Underhill?" he asked.

"I'll do that."

Mariner went out the door while she searched the file for the lawyer's phone number. She dialled, and it took a moment to get through his secretary. Then he came on the line.

"Mr. Underhill, this is Sarah Simonac, the Crown attorney in the case of Charles Abbott."

"It's about time you returned my call." His tone of voice showed his impatience.

"We are all busy, Mr. Underhill."

"My client is in jail!"

"All the cells down here are full. There's nothing special about Abbott. I am calling to tell you that we are going to amend the charges. Then there will be a new bail hearing."

"When?"

"Can you be at Old City Hall in half an hour?"

"Where do I go?"

"Come to the Crown's office."

"And what are the new charges?"

"Dangerous driving causing bodily harm."

"Christ!"

"See you then." She was about to hang up when he asked.

"Will that Detective Mariner be there?"

"Yes."

"Isn't he a piece of work?"

"He is doing his job," and she hung up. She heard complaints against the police all the time from the defence lawyers, and she made a practice of ignoring them.

It was more than an hour before everything was arranged. She had to find a judge who would listen to the case and then find an empty courtroom. Abbott was in a holding cell downstairs. Mariner and Alex waited in the police waiting room. Members of the press were in the hallway outside the courtroom, laughing and cracking jokes with each other. James Underhill paced the corridor. This time he was in his full Bay Street uniform with black pinstripe suit and flowered tie. He was very agitated. Men like him were not usually kept waiting.

Just before they were called inside, Ricky Abbott and his wife, Leona, came rushing in. Underhill had called Ricky about the developments in the case. The three of them had a quick discussion in the corridor.

"They are changing the charges to dangerous driving causing bodily harm," Underhill explained.

"Is that good?" asked Ricky.

"It shows they don't have the evidence to support second-degree murder. It was my pressure that got the charge changed."

"Thank you."

"Once I talked to them, they knew they couldn't get second-degree murder to stick."

"Where is he?"

"In the holding cell."

"The press is here." Ricky Abbott seemed nervous.

"I don't like it any more than you. This is turning into a political football."

"Can the press come into the courtroom?"

"I'm afraid so. These are open courts."

"Christ. That's the last thing I need. I've got a business to run."

"You should be telling that to your brother," said Leona.

"Let's take it calmly," said the lawyer. "I think your brother will get out this afternoon."

"Is he guilty?" Leona asked.

"We will certainly plead not guilty of this charge."

"That's not what I asked."

"Later," said her husband impatiently. "Let's just get him out of this place."

And a moment later they were called into the courtroom. The family, along with their lawyer, went in first, followed by the press. Inside they found the Crown attorney and the two policemen along with the clerk and a stenographer. Charles Abbott came in through a door at the front of the courtroom and stood in the dock beside a prison guard. James Underhill went over to stand beside his client.

"All rise," the clerk announced. Everyone got to their feet, and the judge came sweeping in wearing his black robe. "Judge Norman Taylor presiding." When the judge sat down, it signalled that everyone else could sit. The judge was installed on a raised platform behind an impressive desk. On the wall behind him was the Canadian crest. Flags were mounted on either side of the crest.

"Yes, Ms. Simonac?" the judge asked.

The Crown held papers in her hand as she spoke. "Your Honour, the accused in the dock is Mr. Charles Abbott. He was charged on Friday night with second-degree murder in the death of Ms. Shelly McTavish. That charge has now been withdrawn, and a new charge of dangerous driving causing bodily harm, contrary to Section 249 of the Canadian Criminal Code, has been filed against Mr. Abbott. You will find the papers in your file."

"I didn't do it, Your Honour, sir," Abbott suddenly blurted out.

The judge was not surprised at the outburst. "We are not having a trial today, Mr. Abbott. That will come later. You will have plenty of time to answer the charges."

The judge shuffled through the papers and then nodded towards the Crown. "Yes, I have the papers here. Continue, Ms. Simonac."

"Your Honour, the justice of the peace felt he could not deal with the issue of bail because of the seriousness of the second-degree murder charge. I understand the accused and his lawyer would like to apply for bail. This is Mr. James Underhill. He is Mr. Abbott's lawyer."

"Yes, Mr. Underhill?"

"Your Honour, I am from the law firm of Munro, Stafford and Malone, and we have been engaged to represent Mr. Abbott." Underhill wanted the judge to know he came from one of the most prestigious law firms in the country. "The accused in this case, Mr. Charles Abbott, comes from a well-known family in the city. He works as a salesman for his brother, the businessman Mr. Richard Abbott. He is a very responsible person, with a wife and family that he supports. The law is quite clear that a person may only be held in custody awaiting trial if there is the fear that he or she may abscond or if the accused is a danger to the community. There is no reason to believe that either of these things will happen in this case, and therefore, I would like to request bail for my client."

"I think you will find that this court is quite familiar with the law on bail, Mr. Underhill," the judge said with some sarcasm. "Ms. Simonac, do you oppose bail?"

"Perhaps Detective Mariner would like to respond, Your Honour."

"Detective Mariner, would you come forward, please? "Are you the investigator in this case?

"Yes, Your Honour."

"Tell me your objections."

"Your Honour, this is a very serious charge, and there is evidence of gross neglect. A young woman was killed on the city streets. The public is very concerned that this matter be treated in such a way that is appropriate to the crime. I believe that the accused should be held in custody until such time as the court decides his guilt or innocence. In that way it will demonstrate that public safety in this city is of utmost importance."

The judge looked at the press. Many of them had written down every word of the detective. Abbott, the accused, was flushed and frightened. Sarah Simonac seemed agitated. Only James Underhill exuded a sense of confidence that his argument would prevail. Judge Taylor knew he would be criticized no matter what decision he came to. Everyone in the court listened intently.

"I am setting bail at $100,000, subject to the following conditions. Mr. Abbott, you are to stay in the city of Toronto, you are to continue your employment, abstain from drinking and you are banned from driving while bail is in effect. Do you understand?"

James Underhill was standing beside his client. "Yes, sir. We will comply with those orders."

"I would like to hear it from Mr. Abbott, please."

"Yes, sir. No problem, sir," said the accused.

"Very well." The judge wrote something on a piece a paper and put it in the file while everyone waited. Then he continued. "I agree with Detective Mariner that the public is concerned about this case. For that reason I am remanding the case for three weeks, November 2 at 10 a.m. in this courtroom. The trial will commence at that time. Is that time acceptable, Ms. Simonac?"

She always carried her appointment book with her, and she searched for November 2. "Yes, Your Honour."

"Mr. Underhill?"

"Yes, Your Honour."

"Thank you."

The judge wrote something in the file and then got to his feet. Others in the courtroom stood until he left the room. Sarah Simonac went out of the courtroom and met the reporters in the hallway to make a statement. Mariner and Alex slipped out behind her, unnoticed, and headed back to the police station.

Underhill explained to Ricky Abbott that he would have to pledge the money for the bail.

"One hundred thousand dollars is a lot of money for that brother of yours," was Leona's comment.

CHAPTER 10

When they got back to Division 52 headquarters and signed in, the duty officer phoned Mariner and said that someone was waiting to see him.

"Who?"

"He says he knows something about the accident on Friday night. He's out here in the waiting room with a woman. Been here about two hours."

"Let's hope this is the break we need," Mariner told Alex.

They arranged an interview room, and Alex went out to get them as Mariner waited in the room. When he returned with Spider and Jay, Alex eased the introduction by describing their roles. "This is Detective Mariner. He is the lead investigating officer on the case. I am his partner."

They settled into the chairs, the detectives on one side of the table and Spider and Jay on the other. Mariner conducted the interview, and Alex took notes.

Spider's long hair flowed onto his shoulders. Mariner noticed that the tattoo on his neck disappeared under his heavy canvas shirt and reappeared on the back of his right hand. He wore baggy pants with heavy boots. Jay was dressed simply with a pullover top, pants and boots. Both of them seemed very tense.

"Can we begin by getting your full names, please?" Mariner asked.

"I'm George Smith."

"Tell them what they call you," added Jay.

"Yeah, well, like, Spider. That's what I'm known as on the street. Nobody knows me by George."

"And I'm Jay Rankin."

"You're partners?"

"Yes, sir," Jay answered.

"So tell me why you came in."

Spider combed back his hair with his fingers. "Like, I'm a bike courier, and I was goin' along College on Friday night."

Spider felt a nervous dampness between his shoulder blades. Even being in a police station talking to cops made him anxious. He took a deep breath to help gain control.

Mariner watched him closely. "Did you see the accident?" he asked, trying to help.

"No, no, I wasn't there, but I seen this guy with his big fuckin' car." The swear word had slipped out unintentionally, and that made Spider even more anxious. Swearing in front of police officers just didn't feel right. He glanced again at Jay. He didn't want to make any more mistakes.

"Tell him what happened," Jay offered.

Mariner waited patiently. He had met a lot of men like Spider.

"Like, I was comin' west along College Street because I had to make this delivery, and there was this big SUV up ahead of me. I was ridin' hard 'cause it was seven at night, and I wanted to get home. So I noticed this SUV, and it was all over the road. It came into the bike lane at least three times. Almost hit a guy on a bike up ahead of me."

He paused to collect his thoughts. The policemen waited patiently. "So, like, I got pissed, if you know what I mean." Another swear word, but Spider carried on, gaining confidence as he talked. "So he stopped at one of the traffic lights, and I shouted at him."

"What did you say?"

"I said, 'Stay in your own lane.' Somethin' like that. Like, I thought I should do that. Somebody could get hurt."

Mariner watched him carefully, trying to imagine what Spider would be like on the witness stand. His appearance alone would not give a good impression.

"Did the driver react to your comment?"

"Yeah, I could see him inside his car, and he looked furious. Fat guy, you know, and he got all pink and red. He began rolling down the window on the passenger side. I guess the car had those automatic window things. Know what I mean? But I didn't want to get into trouble. Not with him. Not with nobody. So I took off. I went through the red light. I know I'm not supposed to but…. And so I was headin' west along the bike path there."

"Where were you at that time?"

"I was comin' up to the Dovercourt light. Maybe a couple of blocks before it. And so I was ridin' along, thinking it was over, when suddenly this big, fuckin' car.... Oh, sorry about that."

"That's okay. Go on."

"This car, the big SUV, it pulls over toward me, forcing me up against the curb. Pointed his car right across the bike lane, and he was shouting at me out the window. I had to jam on my brakes or I would have hit him. So, you know, I was upset. Like, really pissed off, and so I put my bike up against a pole or somethin', and I was gonna sort him out. Like, not hit him or nothin' like that. I told him he shouldn't be comin' into the bike lane 'cause he could hit somebody."

"Did you shout at him?"

"Well, yeah, because I was steamed. Know what I mean? But I wasn't gonna do him or nothin' like that. I just told him he could hurt someone." And he glanced at Jay again, trying to sense the impression he was giving.

"What did he say to you?"

"He said... he said," and Spider glanced at Jay again. "He told me to f... off. That roads are for cars, not bikes. Stuff like that."

Spider was intense, and his description gave Mariner a feeling of the heat of the moment he was describing—the rising anger of the two men, Spider, lean and tall and fit from hours of hard riding every day; Abbott, fat and indolent from spending his time sitting in cars or behind a desk. He nodded at Spider to continue.

"So I got around to the driver's side, and I said something more. Like, I guess I was hot, and he could see that, and he panicked. He must have stepped on the accelerator, and the car jumped ahead. Its back wheels were screaming, and the car went up on the curb and onto the sidewalk. Then he must have pulled on the steering wheel, and the car came back onto the road. He had to jam on the brakes or he would have hit another car in his lane just up ahead. I mean, he could have killed somebody right there. He was out of control. You've gotta understand that."

Mariner was nodding. This was what they needed if they were to get a conviction.

Spider continued. "I had to get out of there. Like, he was too much trouble for me. He was a fuckin' maniac. You know, like.... So after he took off, I got back on my bike, and I crossed the street and went up to the corner and then went south on Dovercourt. I never saw him again."

"So you never saw the accident."

"I was long gone when it happened. I didn't hear about it till Saturday night, and I was watchin' television with my girlfriend, Jay here, and they had a picture of the man. What's his name?"

"Abbott."

"Yeah, and they had a picture of the car. That's when I remembered everything. So what must have happened was that he didn't know that I went across the street or nothin', and as he came up to the light he must have been watchin' in his mirror on the right-hand side of the car, and he saw the girl comin' along in the bike lane, only he thought it was me. So he said to himself, I'm gonna get that son of a bitch, and he timed it—watchin' the girl, watchin' the light, and just at the moment when she was almost beside him, he turned hard right at the corner. The girl hit the side of the car, and he ran over her."

"So you think he was trying to kill you."

"Yeah, it has to be that."

Mariner ran Spider's description through his mind. Abbott is angry and wants revenge. He watches the figure get larger in the mirror, waiting until he thinks Spider is right beside him. Then, at the right moment, he makes a sudden right turn. He intended to kill Spider, or at least hurt him, but he killed the girl by mistake. The explanation made sense. The only problem was it could never be used in court. It was no more than speculation.

"Well, Spider, this is very interesting," said the detective. "Do you have anything to add?"

"I don't think so. After that I made the delivery and went home. I didn't think of it again until, like I said, I was watchin' TV on Saturday night."

"Are you prepared to make a statement about all of this?"

Spider began to feel uneasy again. He glanced at Jay, and she was nodding. "Yeah, sure."

"And are you prepared to be a witness in a court of law and be cross-examined by lawyers?"

His hands swept through his hair. In that moment of panic, he remembered what it was like at his own trial for dealing dope. Friends told him to plead not guilty. They said the cops don't have any evidence, and so when he got on the stand he tried to lie his way out of it, only the Crown tore his story apart and found every one of his distortions. Spider could still hear the lawyer's words. "You are nothing but a liar! I don't believe a word you are saying!" The judge agreed with the Crown and that added to his sentence. God, he just needed to put all of that shit behind him.

"Do I have to go to court?"

"I expect Abbott will plead not guilty. That means there will be a trial, and you will have to testify if you want this evidence to be taken into account."

Mariner watched the agony on Spider's face. Even his body was twitching with nervousness. Men like this didn't even know why they felt such panic when they faced authority.

"Is there something you would like to tell me, Spider?" Mariner could predict what was coming.

"Like … I've got a record."

Mariner nodded but said nothing.

"Do you think that might come up in the court?"

"It might."

Spider closed his eyes. "Jesus," was all he could say. The whole torment came back to him. He was breathing hard, trying to calm himself. Jay leaned forward and put her hand in his. She wanted to hold him and ease his vulnerability.

"Like, I've got a record for dealin' dope and other stuff. I did two years less a day."

Mariner nodded. "Do you still want to testify?"

Spider looked at Jay. God, they'd both been trying to stay off the booze and the drugs, but it was hard. So fuckin' hard. And now this. Being up there on the witness stand with the lawyers goin' at him. Jesus, why did it have to be him? But Jay was with him. He could feel her power. He'd be nothing without her. He couldn't do it. He'd be doin' smack in a back alley within a week if he didn't have her. Homeless. Drunk. And if he went down this time, he'd never climb out again. Never.

He looked at this cop watching him patiently. Waiting. He wasn't pushing him. He was just waiting for him to make up his mind, like he believed that he was a man, an adult, who was in possession of his life. It was up to him to decide.

"Yeah," he said. His mouth was so dry it came out almost as a whisper.

"What's that?" Mariner leaned forward to hear.

Spider breathed deeply. "I said, yes. I will go on the witness stand." He had made up his mind, and now he felt in control.

Mariner spoke calmly. "All you have to do is tell the truth, Spider. Don't invent things that didn't happen. It's not up to you to judge Abbott, or decide who is to blame for the girl's death. That's up to the judge. All you have to do to help him is tell the truth."

"What if they bring up all that stuff about all of my convictions?"

"Just tell the truth. That's all you can do. Let the judge decide what is right or wrong, or what is relevant or irrelevant."

"Will what I say make a difference?"

"I think it will. Your story is an important part of the puzzle as to what happened to Shelly McTavish. Most people think that finding out what happened should be easy, but I can tell you, sometimes, finding out the truth is the most difficult thing in the world. So, yes, your testimony will be very important in this case."

"What happens now?" Jay asked.

"My partner has taken notes, and the two of us will write it into a statement. Do you have a phone, Spider?"

"Yeah, a mobile. I need it for my work." He held it up for them to see.

"Give us the number. We will phone you when the statement is prepared. I want you to come in and read it. Jay, you can come, too, if you like. This is your statement,

Spider, and I want you to make it accurate. If you agree with it, then I would like you to sign it. Both the Crown and the defence lawyers will see the statement, and they will be able to ask you questions about it in the trial."

"Okay."

"And I want you to keep November 2 aside. Put it on your calendar. That is the day when the trial will happen, and I expect you will be an important witness. Is there anything else?"

"No, no, I don't think so."

Mariner got to his feet to indicate the interview was over. "Thank you for coming in." He held out his hand and Spider took it. "I know this must be difficult for you."

"Like Jay says, the girl, she was killed. Like, she was a mother and everything. It's just not right."

"I agree. It's not right."

Alex took them through the maze of rooms and hallways to the front entrance. When he returned, he found Mariner sitting at his desk gazing into space. "What do you think?" he asked.

"No, you tell me what you think, Alex."

"He's not going to be a credible witness. Just the way he presents himself and his record...."

"But he tells the truth, and he is the only witness we have who can provide a glimpse into Abbott's motivation."

"But we can't use all that stuff about Abbott trying to kill him, rather than the girl."

"I know, but with Spider's testimony we've got evidence of Abbott's erratic driving, and that he was endangering other cyclists. The other witnesses will corroborate that. That means we should be able to get a dangerous driving conviction."

"But no one will believe a guy like Spider."

"We'll see."

CHAPTER 11

The next day Sarah Simonac was impossibly busy. She was arguing an illegal possession of firearms case at 10 o'clock. Then she had a meeting with the court administrator to go over the pending cases. At some point in the day she had to check on the part-time Crowns to see if she could solve problems before they became real headaches. She knew some of the Crowns were incompetent, but what could she do? They were all political appointments. On top of all this, there was the case of the woman cyclist.

It was still in the headlines. She didn't have time to see the television coverage, but she read two newspapers when she got into work and accounts of the bail hearing were on the front pages of both of them. She was quoted extensively. Again, the stories were accompanied by photos of Shelly McTavish with her baby in her arms. The photos gave an intimate glimpse into the victim's life, and Sarah knew that these images would create a collective sense of anger through the city.

But the big news was the mayor's press conference the previous morning. He didn't seem to care that he was only stirring up the issue. Or maybe he was cleverly using the death as a way to underline that he was not going to spend any more on bike lanes. The press conference was about transit spending, but the reporters insisted on getting the mayor's reaction to the killing of the young mother.

"Look," he was quoted in both papers as saying, "The streets are for cars and trucks. They are dangerous for cyclists."

"Are you saying it was her fault?" one of the reporters asked.

"Cyclists are taking their lives in their hands when they go out on the streets."

"But your opponents on council say streets are for everyone, and cars and trucks have to share the roads with cyclists. And they say the city could do much more to protect cyclists by providing concrete barriers for the cycling lanes."

"We can't afford it," was the mayor's answer, and with that he left the press conference.

The whole thing was a political football, and the Crown knew that the courts were caught in the middle. It was now clear that this would be a prominent case, and she would have to handle it in court because she couldn't trust the other Crown counsel who worked for her.

She would show complete impartiality on the political issues of the case, but she couldn't help but have her own opinion. She either walked to work or took the streetcar and subway. She didn't own a car, and she didn't cycle either, but lot of her friends rode their bikes to work every day. Why couldn't the streets be designed for cyclists as well as cars?

But that wasn't her business. Leave it to the politicians. She was running a big operation, and the last thing she needed was to get caught up in politics. She had learned as a Crown to separate her own feelings and opinions from what she was working on.

At times that was very hard. Every day she saw people in crisis in the courtrooms: women beaten up by drunken husbands, 19-year-olds hooked on heroin with a pregnant girlfriend facing dozens of charges of break and entry, kids dealing drugs, caught in the gang wars that raged in the city. If she became involved emotionally in these cases, she couldn't do her job.

Justice. She remembered debating that in a moot court in law school, but that was so long ago now that she couldn't even remember the arguments. All she could do was focus on her work, keep the cases turning over, hope the adversarial system would ferret out the truth, and the judges had enough sense to impose reasonable sentences on the guilty.

Already at 8:30 that morning she had been delivered a lecture by one of the judges complaining about the way one of her lawyers had handled a case. She promised to speak to the Crown about it, but really she had just listened and let it roll off her back. What could she do? All the Crowns were lawyers. They were professionals. It wasn't up to her to tell them how to handle their cases. And why didn't the judges complain about the defence lawyers? There was a real problem, but they were independent, and there was no way the judges could touch them.

When she got back to her office, she barely had time to check her messages before she had to get into court. There was another message from James Underhill. "Please phone me back." *To hell with him,* she thought. She wasn't going to help a Bay Street lawyer satisfy his client. But there was one thing she had to do before she went into court.

She grabbed her phone, punched in the numbers and waited until Mariner came on the line.

"Sarah Simonac here."

"How you doin'?"

"Busy as hell. Look, this Abbott case is front-page news. I want our side to look good when it comes to trial 'cause the press will be all over it."

"Yeah."

"So what's the evidence look like?"

"We have witnesses who saw the accident. We know in detail what happened. We've got photographs, the works, and now we have a witness who can testify that Abbott was driving dangerously as he drove along College Street."

"Good. How credible are the witnesses?"

"Most are excellent. One's a little shaky."

"What's the problem?"

"He's got a criminal record."

"Do we need him?"

"Yeah."

"Try to find someone else."

"He'll be fine."

"Okay. I want you to put it all together, and we'll meet a couple of days before the trial. I want to get a conviction. Understand?"

"Never can tell what a judge might think."

"I just want us to look good because the press is going to be all over this case. I don't want a story saying the Crown or the police bungled it."

"It won't happen on our end."

"If you've got the goods, I can deliver them. I'll call you back to set up the time to meet."

"Okay."

She hung up, grabbed her file and headed out to the courtroom where the firearms case was to be heard. By the time she got back to her office about noon, she felt wrung out. The defence had put the accused's wife on the stand, and she burst into tears, declaring her family would fall apart if her husband went to jail. Sarah had to argue this had nothing to do with the guilt or innocence of the accused. By the time the case was over, she was convinced that the defence counsel didn't even understand points of evidence in a criminal case. He should go back to closing house deals, not dealing with people's lives, she thought.

In the office she found another message from Underhill. This time she felt she couldn't ignore him any longer and phoned him back. Once she got through his secretary, he came on the line.

"I was hoping we could catch lunch together." Underhill was using all of his charm. "The lunch is on me."

"I'm very busy. I usually work through lunch." There was nothing wrong with lawyers discussing cases before the trial. In fact, the judges liked it when the two sides could work out a settlement that would avoid lengthy trials, but Sarah knew that Underhill had a motive. Anyway, she was not sure she wanted to have lunch with him. He was too Bay Street for her.

"That's too bad. You've got to get away from work sometimes."

"We don't all work for big law firms with a budget for lunches." She laughed, but she knew Underhill would recognize that this was an intentional dig. "What do you want to discuss?"

"Our case, of course. Abbott."

"Things usually calm down around here about four. You work just down the street from the Old City Hall courts. Why don't you come to my office around then?"

"Fine. I'll see you then."

She knew she had done the right thing. Better to get him to come into her turf then to feel a sense of obligation after he bought her lunch. Underhill was different from the other lawyers who defended cases at Old City Hall. They knew the routine and accepted the rules. He was new at the gritty practice of criminal law.

Underhill arrived promptly at four. Sarah was only partway through her paperwork. It would keep her in the office until seven that night. She led off with small talk.

"You're not usually around the Old City Hall law courts."

"I had a case here the first year I was practising. I think it was a drunk driving case."

"Then the Highway Safety Act must be your specialty." She said with a smile. "That pays the bills for a lot of lawyers."

"Hardly. I work in a big corporate law firm, and I get to litigate civil cases."

"I expect that is a little more lucrative than the sort of things that we get down here."

"I guess we work in the area that interests us."

Sarah knew that defence lawyers took the cases that came their way. If you had a small practice with no secretary, you defended kids up on charges of theft or assault, wife beaters and drunk and disorderly. "Poverty law" they called it to dress it up a little, and poverty was the income of lawyers who had clients like this. If you worked at a corporate law office you got corporate clients and a high income.

"How did you get the Abbott case?"

"Through his brother. His company is a client of our firm. Not a big one, but big enough."

At least Sarah didn't have to worry about finding clients. There was an unending line-up of people coming through the courts who required prosecution by a Crown attorney. "It can't be easy dealing with a client like that."

"The problem is, who's the client? Is it Ricky, who pays the fee, or is it Chuckie, who's in trouble with the law?" Underhill laughed at his predicament.

"Sounds like there is a little tension there."

"No, not really. Both of them are determined to get a fair trial with the best outcome."

"A fair trial they'll get, but they might not like the outcome."

"I don't believe that's the case."

"Why not?"

"I don't think the charge that has been laid is the correct one."

She had seen it coming, and she was prepared for it. "The whole city is up in arms about this case. No one here is going to walk away from it."

"But in essence it is just a simple traffic accident."

"I don't think it is so simple. There is the question of intent, and the case plays into the controversy about the safety of bicycles in the city that has been going on for months. Now a young mother has been killed. Everyone will watch this case very closely."

"But that controversy has been put to rest. When the mayor was elected, we all knew his policy on traffic and cycling."

"It's not been put to rest at all, and this case has given ammunition to the cyclists. The mayor now is on the defensive. The issue is spinning out of control."

"But the whole thing is just an overheated political argument. The law is supposed to be above all that."

"Yeah, but it never is."

"It should be."

"Look we try, but judges and Crown attorneys read newspapers. They are part of the community, and controversies like this have an influence on the courts. You know that. It can't be helped."

"You are seriously questioning the impartiality of the court?"

"I'm saying I live in the real world. But I have confidence in the courts. I see them at work every day. The judges do the best they possibly can. It's not a perfect world, you know."

"Well, you know, all this just leads to my conclusion that we need a more appropriate charge. This dangerous driving causing bodily harm is just playing into the political controversy, and it's not realistic. This is simply an accident where an unfortunate woman was killed. It happens every day. We should not be swept up into some political crusade. Our responsibility is to be objective and fair. If we want to see justice to be done we should find a more appropriate charge."

"What would you suggest?"

"The dangerous driving charge should be dropped and a new charge of careless driving laid. That is much more appropriate."

"And a much-less-serious charge."

"But it is appropriate to the circumstances. That's my point. I can tell you that if the charge is reduced to careless driving, I will recommend that my client plead guilty, but we will fight the dangerous driving charge all the way. What is more, I will argue in the court that the dangerous driving charge was politically motivated."

Sarah laughed. "That's a little rich."

"You as much as said so yourself. You said in a case such as this, the courts get swept away by the overheated politics of the day. In court I will argue that the political climate led to the laying of an inappropriate charge, I won't say it was malicious or anything like that. Let's call it an unintended consequence of the politics of the day."

Now Sarah was on her guard. Had she gone too far in idle lawyer speculation about the influence of politics on the courts? "You will find that argument will not go far in the criminal courts practised in the Old City Hall."

"Oh, but there are appeal courts, as you know."

"Rather than reduce the charge, perhaps the original charge of second-degree murder is more appropriate."

"I think you recognize yourself that charge that would be impossible to win. That's why you changed it to dangerous driving."

"We have very strong witnesses who will testify that Abbott was driving dangerously and almost hit other people."

"I can see you are relying on Detective Mariner. I would be very careful of him. He is on a witch hunt against my client."

"A witch hunt?"

"Well, maybe that is a little strong." Underhill realized he had overplayed his hand in the heat of the discussion. Maybe Mariner was a friend of the Crown. "But I know that dangerous driving is inappropriate."

The conversation was annoying Sarah, but if she showed it he would see it as a victory. "As you said, criminal law is not your specialty, Mr. Underhill," she said with some sarcasm.

"Call me Jamie, please."

"If you did practise it on a regular basis, you would know that dangerous driving causing bodily harm is exactly the right charge in this case. When you read our evidence, you will understand that we have witnesses who can testify that Abbott was driving in a dangerous and irresponsible way. We could have proceeded with the second-degree murder charge. There certainly is evidence of gross negligence. I would have been willing to proceed on that basis, but in the end I decided to reduce the charge to dangerous driving. I am certainly not going to reduce it to careless driving."

"But don't you see that forces you to establish neglect, and that is a very high bar."

"I think I understand the law, Mr. Underhill. Particularly the criminal law and how it is practised in this court."

Underhill had played all of his cards, but he tried one last time. "You know very well that the courts want lawyers to try to avoid lengthy litigation. If you agree to reduce the charge to careless driving, I will agree that my client will plead guilty. Then it will be over. If not, then I am afraid we could face lengthy court proceedings."

Sarah got to her feet to let him know the conversation was at an end. "Then I am afraid, Mr. Underhill, I will see you in court on November 2."

They parted on reasonable terms. Lawyers have remarkable skills to manoeuvre through tense social situations. But the line had been drawn, and both understood that there would be an intensely fought courtroom battle.

CHAPTER 12

Mariner looked up Spider's record in the police database. It did not look good. George Smith, alias Spider. A quick calculation of his date of birth made him 21 years of age. A photo taken when he was 19, and arrested for the trafficking charge, was in the right-hand corner of the page. He looked totally wasted.

There was a long list of convictions with a date beside each of the occurrences: assault, break and enter, possession of marijuana, assault, trafficking in an illegal substance. It was the trafficking charge that got him two years less a day. Spider had spent lengthy periods of time in jail awaiting trial for all of these offences. That meant the judges didn't want him on the street. There was a note saying Spider had a lengthy record as a young offender, but that list of offences was not in the file. The law said that convictions of a young offender could not be used in trials when the individual became an adult and could not be released to the public.

What Mariner found interesting was that there were no criminal convictions since Spider had been sent to prison. On another page of the digital file was a note that he had been charged with threatening two months before, but no conviction was registered. He followed the reference and found the occurrence report. It was written by Detective Jim McKay, a policeman Mariner had known for years.

The report described an argument between Spider and another bike courier that got out of hand and ended in a fight. The police were called. Witnesses said that Spider had caused the fight, but the courier who had been assaulted refused to press charges. McKay had laid the charge because of Spider's long record. The judge for some reason decided to give Spider a discharge, without registering a conviction, on the condition that he attend a therapist once a week and report to a probation officer.

A conditional discharge was unusual for someone with a lengthy criminal record like Spider's. It could mean that the judge thought it was a bogus charge, or maybe Spider gave a good account of himself and convinced the judge that he was going to stay out of trouble.

Jim McKay worked out of 51 Division, one of the roughest parts of the city, with most of the hostels and dozens of rooming houses. He was known as good-natured guy, but a "cop's cop," tough and unyielding, someone who knew how to handle the drunks and addicts who lived in the east end. Mariner phoned him. It took a couple of days before they were able to connect because of the shift rotations, but finally McKay returned the call.

"Do they still have you out there in the west end Mariner?" McKay said over the phone.

"'Fraid so."

"Hangin' out with the party boys in the Entertainment District and the Chinks in Chinatown," and he laughed.

Mariner remembered why he had never liked McKay very much, but he was not going to protest the racist remark. "I hear you know a guy by the name of Spider Smith. George Spider Smith."

"Know him? Christ, I've arrested that son of a bitch more times than I've been laid in the last two years. What's he done now?"

"Nothing, as it happens. I want to use him as a witness in the case of the young woman cyclist killed up on College Street."

"Are you nuts? Have you talked to Spider?"

"Yeah."

"He's a fuckin' heroin addict."

"Is he still on the hard stuff?"

"Ever seen any of those guys get off it?"

"A few."

"Jesus, Mariner. Get real. A guy like Spider's never going to make it. I've known that kid since he was 16, when I was just transferred into 51 Division. I must have arrested him three times when he was still a young adult. I set up the trafficking charge. He was selling dope out of a doughnut shop at Dundas and Sherbourne, so I sent this young recruit in, and he bought some heroin from him. He came out with the stuff, and the next thing Spider knew I was there putting the cuffs on him. Easiest takedown I've ever done. I found out later that he was so spaced out on the junk they had to call a doctor to bring him down easy. That's what sort of a guy he is."

"What's his background like?"

"I knew his mother. God knows where his father is. Prison, most likely. His mother used to turn tricks out along Jarvis Street. She could have been an addict, too. I don't know. They used to live in a two-room place over on Sackville Street. That kid will never be out of trouble."

"What about the threatening charge where he was given a conditional discharge?"

"Christ, he had only been out of jail a couple of weeks, and he got this job working as a bike courier. They don't care who they hire. He's got a bad temper, I've seen it myself, and he got into a fight with another courier. The guy didn't want to lay charges against Spider, so I did it myself. And you know, I couldn't believe it, he got a young judge who decided to give him a discharge on the condition that he go to a therapist. A lot of good that will do. Can you imagine a guy like Spider listening to a therapist?"

"That was a couple of months ago. He hasn't been in trouble since."

"You wait. Spider can't stay out of trouble for long. You've seen guys like that, Mariner, same as me."

"I don't know. It looks like he's trying."

"It's the booze and the drugs that get these guys. He'll go in to have a beer, and the next thing you know he's shooting heroin."

"My sense is he hasn't been on the hard stuff since he went inside."

"Did he tell you that?"

"No. It's just a feeling I have."

McKay laughed. "You're still the soft-hearted cop, Mariner. You'd believe the devil himself if he said he was going straight." And he laughed again.

Mariner laughed with him. That was his reputation, and he wasn't ashamed of it.

"Look, I've gotta go," said McKay. "A couple of kids rolled a drunk last night. Stole 10 bucks from him.

They're up in juvenile court this morning. Never stops, you know. Nothing ever changes. There's always a fresh bunch of punks coming along looking for trouble. But you know, Mariner, I wouldn't put Spider on the stand. No way. The lawyer will ask him a couple of questions, and he'll lose it. Anger management is what they call it now. What a laugh. He's got a bad-ass temper, that's all." And he signed off.

Mariner smiled to himself. "Big Jim McKay" they used to call him when they worked together. He was a happy-go-lucky guy who loved to talk. He never changed. McKay was always convinced that kids in trouble with the law were heading for the slammer, and there was no hope for reform. Mariner never accepted that.

The same day he looked through Spider's file he searched for Charles Abbott in the data base. The rule was that information on an accused's criminal record could not be used prior to conviction because it might prejudice the judge, but it was entered in the record once a conviction was made. This file was rich in detail.

There was a drunk driving conviction three years before. A year before that he had a careless driving conviction that involved an accident. Interesting—two fairly serious driving offences and now this dangerous driving charge. This guy had problems, and if convicted on the latest offence he could do some serious time.

But the most interesting thing in the file had nothing to do with driving. In the same month as the drunk driving conviction, Abbott had been convicted of assault causing bodily harm in a domestic dispute. He had assaulted his wife and broken her jaw. He was arrested and spent the night in jail. The next morning, his brother bailed him out, but the justice of the peace stipulated in the conditions of bail that Abbott was to live with his brother, he was not allowed to see his wife or his children and could not visit the home. A month later, he was convicted of the assault charge.

Attached to the file was a scanned copy of the arresting officer's report of the offence, written in longhand. It was hard to decipher, and Mariner had to read it a couple of times to make out everything. The report was written by P.C. William Young, and it provided much more detail than the normal occurrence reports. Young was obviously upset by what he saw.

> My partner, P.C. Peter O'Brien, and I were dispatched to the home of Mr. Charles Abbott in North York, at 11:30 p.m. When we arrived at the house, the front door stood open. We heard moaning sounds that indicated that someone was injured, and we entered the premises.
>
> Mrs. Jennifer Abbott lay on the floor bleeding profusely from her mouth. Mr. Charles Abbott was sitting on the couch. He appeared to be extremely intoxicated and agitated.
>
> P.C. O'Brien went out to our police car parked on the street to call for an ambulance while I stayed in the house. Mrs. Abbott appeared to be in considerable pain. I tried to assist her, but she indicated that she did not want me to touch her on the face or anywhere on her person.
>
> Mr. Abbott continued to curse and shout. I was concerned that he might assault his wife again. He attempted to get up from

the chesterfield, and I pushed him down. Then he directed a steady stream of abuse at me. I tried to put handcuffs on him to ensure that he would not assault his wife again, but I was unable to do so. He is very fat and I could not pin him down and get the cuffs on him. Shortly thereafter my partner returned, and together we were able to get the handcuffs on him.

While this was going on I noticed two young children standing on the stairway watching. They were crying. Once we got the handcuffs on Mr. Abbott, the children rushed to their mother and held onto her.

Meanwhile, Mr. Abbott continued to use verbally abusive language against his wife and then against the children. Both P.C. O'Brien and I told him to stop, but he continued.

Shortly thereafter the paramedics arrived and attended to Mrs. Abbott. This made the children even more upset. Mr. Abbott tried to strike out at his wife and children again, and we had to restrain him.

Detectives arrived as Mrs. Abbott was taken out of the house. They phoned the Children's Aid Society. They then ordered P.C. O'Brien and me to take Mr. Abbott down to the station, which we did.

Mr. Abbott attempted to assault P.C. O'Brien and myself, but I would not recommend a charge of assault police.

He was charged assault causing bodily harm and lodged in a cell in 32 Division.

Mariner made notes on the report and then turned off the computer. He pushed his chair back, trying to imagine what it was like that night in the Abbott household. When he was in uniform he had been sent to scenes like this maybe six or seven times. They were among the most disturbing things that he had witnessed as a police officer. It was obvious that Constable Young had been very upset as he was writing his report.

The public believed that the police were out on the streets playing cops and robbers or solving puzzling murder cases. The ugly truth was that family violence like this was often the work they were required to do.

Mariner knew the pattern. Alcohol had a lot to do with it, but it was likely to be a combination of many things. The husband's work isn't going well, and his dreams as a young man are turning sour. Financial problems often are a part of it. The couple constantly bicker with each other. She is angry because she is trapped at home with the kids while he cruises the bars. Out of frustration, she uses the only weapons she has. She calls him names: he's a loser; he'll never amount to anything. It goes on for weeks … months.

Then one evening he is invited out for drinks by friends or people at work. One drink turns into five. No one can blame the guy if he gets a little drunk, they say. He's under a lot of pressure. Then there are more drinks, and he finally heads home.

He drives home. Guys like this always drive home. They have heard the advertising about drinking and driving, but they've got to get home, and they can't leave the car behind. If he's lucky, the police see him and pull him over for driving erratically. He spends the night in jail and faces a drunk driving charge, but at least he doesn't beat up his wife that night. Most times, though, he manages to manoeuvre through the streets and arrives home drunk and barely in control.

His wife is angry, so angry this time that she can't stop herself. She has been angry all night, knowing he was going to come home drunk. Hasn't she told him about this over and over again, but he never listens. He's no good. He never thinks of her or the kids. Their life that started with such promise, such hope, such love, has turned to this. She can't stand it anymore. She screams out her abuse at him, and what makes her words stinging is that he knows deep down that every word is true.

And then it happens. It all explodes in one moment of blinding rage that he can't stop, can't control. He flails out in his anger, and in that moment his life changes irrevocably and nothing will ever be the same again.

The marriage is finished. It's over for all of them, over for his relationship with his wife, over for his relationship with his kids. Everything is over.

She ends up living in a string of rented apartments with the children, struggling with poverty, but at least she is safe, she tells herself. And he is on his way down. Rooming houses, meals in fast-food restaurants, more bars and drinking. Soon he will lose his job, and then the fall is so fast it is like he has walked off the edge of a cliff.

A few can change. There may still be enough love in the relationship that they can make a break from the past. If he is strong, he will end up in AA. Mariner knew Alcoholics Anonymous had saved more marriages and lives than all of the therapists combined. Maybe she can forgive him for the violence and the drunken nights. But it's hard to change. Mariner knew that. He had been married twice and one thing he had learned is that it is extremely hard for anyone to change.

And what happened to the Charles Abbott family after that terrible night? Mariner could guess. He didn't go to AA. The family was finished. The wife and kids would be trying to subsist on welfare and the monthly payments the court forced Abbott to make. The kids would be unhappy and drifting. They were the real victims of the crime.

But Abbott was also a walking wounded. Mariner had no sympathy for him. He didn't like one thing about him; he was responsible for his own life, and he had thrown it away. But still he was a casualty. Hated by his wife and children, dependent on his brother for a job and his livelihood; even the car he drove belonged to his brother's company. All he had left was bluff and bluster that was hollow and meaningless. He was a time bomb waiting to go off—angry, lost, without purpose, and the unfortunate victim was Shelly McTavish, a young woman filled with hope and promise of a spectacular life.

Mariner stirred. It was too depressing even for him. Maybe he was wrong. Maybe the picture he had sketched was distorted, but all of his experience led him to believe that Abbott was a pathetic shell of a man, and that was the real cause of the death of Shelly McTavish.

CHAPTER 13

Charles Abbott was still at work. It had been a difficult month, but in three more days he'd be up in front of the judge, and it would be all over. Or at least he hoped it would be all over.

Someone had told him about a person they knew who faced a dangerous driving charge, and he was sent to jail. *Goddamn, that couldn't happen to me,* he thought. *It was only a fuckin' accident, after all. Anyone could see that. The woman should have seen me.*

Anyway, would the judge have given me bail and let me out on the street if he was gonna sentence me to jail time? No way! Still, he was worried, and he had been worried since he was in court. It was hanging over his head and that added to his tension.

The worst part was that his name was all over the papers. *Jesus, that must have been hard on Ricky. After all, he ran a legit business. Christ, he was an engineer and a millionaire several times over. The Refrigerator Man is what the papers called him, and now the name Abbott had been in the papers over and over again. It was just not right.*

The accident had stirred up the controversy about cycling, and every time it was mentioned the picture of the girl with her baby in her arms was published along with the picture of him taken as he came out of the courtroom. *God, the picture makes me look like a criminal. Why did they have to use that picture anyway?*

The press was just trying to whip up the public against him. It must have been that Detective Mariner. Whenever Charlie saw a news article about it, he felt like shouting, "It was just a fucking accident! An accident, can't you get that through your thick head?"

Only he didn't say that because he only saw the newspapers in the company cafeteria, and it was always filled with other company employees. At least none of them had mentioned the accident to him. Just as well. He might have lost his cool. Still, it seemed they often looked at him in a funny kind of way.

That's why when Joe, the guy who was head of shipping, invited him out for a drink, he accepted. He wanted him to know everything was under control, and maybe Joe wanted Charlie to know that he still thought he was still an okay guy. They agreed to meet down the street at the new Irish pub half an hour after work.

Except there was the problem of getting there. Charlie didn't want to bum a ride with Joe because then he would have to give an explanation. He couldn't say that there was a court order that he could not drive. What would he think?

What a fuckin' nuisance. Here he was having to take the bus to work while his SUV sat in the company parking lot. He still carried the keys in his pocket, but he couldn't drive the damned thing.

He hated the bus. He had to wait at the bus stop for what seemed like hours, and then he was crammed in with all the people. Women, mostly immigrants—refugees—you could see it. There were blacks and Chinese. God, they were all losers, and here he was squished in with them while they chattered away with each other in some foreign language. *Why couldn't they speak English? Probably too stupid to learn.*

But how was he going to get to the pub? He didn't want the guys to see him arrive by bus. *I could call a taxi,* he thought, *but what the fuck. I've got the keys in my pocket. No one will ever know. Even if someone from the company saw me in the car, they wouldn't think anything of it. It is my car, for Christ's sake, or at least it is the company's car, and it's mine to drive.*

He worked a half-hour past quitting time, then got his stuff, slipped out the back door, into the car and out of the parking lot before anyone saw him. It sure felt good to be behind the wheel of the big SUV again. The engine purred. All of the power he ever needed was just a touch away.

He parked in behind the Irish pub and went in through the back door. Joe was already there, along with two other guys from the company. One worked in production, but Charlie couldn't remember his name. And then there was Johnny, who was in sales, like him. He knew them all, and every last one was a good guy. They welcomed him like a brother.

First Charlie had a pint of beer, then a second with a whisky chaser. It was only when the third beer was set before him that he began to relax and feel like his old self again. He began to talk. Charlie liked to talk, and he liked an audience.

They talked about the company and the slump in sales that the company always experienced in November and December. Then Joe asked Charlie about his picture in the paper. He phrased it as a backhanded compliment.

"Jesus, Charlie, you're gettin' famous. Every time I open the paper, there's your picture."

The others were silent. This was the boss's brother, and he faced serious charges. They had all read the newspapers and talked about it among themselves, but it was the first time that Charlie had any idea they knew anything about it.

He tried to downplay it. "What a fuckin' joke, you know? Like, it was just an accident, but the cops have blown it all out of proportion."

"Cops do that all the time," said Joe.

"Wanna watch out for them around here," added the guy from production. "They nailed a friend of mine for drunk driving just down the street."

"I wasn't drunk or nothing like that. They gave me the breathalyzer test and I passed, but this cop got involved, and he's out to get me, if you know what I mean?"

"What'd they charge you with?"

"Dangerous driving causing bodily harm."

"Jesus, that's serious," said Johnny. "I didn't realize it was that serious."

"I know someone who got charged with dangerous driving," added the guy who worked in production. "He got six months in jail."

"Go way!" said Joe.

"Yeah, six months. The guy lost his job and everything."

"No way they're gonna send me down for six months," said Charlie with determination. He drained the rest of his beer and called for another.

The guys drifted away. The one from production said he had to pick up his wife from work. A few minutes later, Joe and Johnny were ready to leave.

"Are you sure you're okay?" asked Joe before he left.

"I'm good."

"Maybe you should take a taxi home, Charlie."

"I'll be all right."

"Don't want to get stopped, particularly if you've got this dangerous driving charge hangin' over your head."

"I'm just gonna finish this one and head out of here."

"Okay," and then Joe and Johnny said goodbye, leaving Charlie at the table nursing his fourth pint of beer.

Nice guys, Charlie thought. He glanced at his watch. It was already pushing seven. Good to get out with the guys again. Just to relax and knock back some cold ones. He used to do that with Ricky all the time, but it stopped after they both got married.

Wonder if there's any truth to the story about the guy getting six months in jail for dangerous driving? No fuckin' way. It couldn't happen to me. It was just a goddamn accident. She should have seen him turning the corner. I signalled my turn. I always signal, and I must have done it that time too.

It's that Detective Mariner, son of a bitch. He's just gunning for a guy like me. But I've got this big lawyer, James Underhill. Even his name sounds impressive. He works for a Bay Street law firm. He's twice as smart as that woman Crown. What the fuck does she know anyway? She works for the government. That's what a loser she is. Anyway, in two days it'll all be cleaned up. Tomorrow, Ricky and I will go down to meet Underhill. Then the next day in court I'll be free and clear.'

Charlie had just ordered another pint from the waitress when Ricky came into the pub. He looked around. Then he spotted Charlie sitting alone at the table. He was very agitated.

Ricky strode across the room. "How long have you been here?" he demanded. "I've been looking all over for you."

"Sit down, Ricky. Have a beer."

"You're not supposed to drink! How can you be so stupid?"

"They'll never know."

"You've got a court order saying you're not supposed to drive, and you took the SUV out of the parking lot! You're not supposed to drink or drive!" Ricky was always in control, but now he was so upset his face was flushed and anger showed in his voice.

"The cops will never find out."

"I've signed a bond for you for $100,000. I'm responsible, you asshole!"

"Don't call me an asshole."

"What do you want me to call you? I mean, Christ, Charlie. I was heading home, and I noticed that your SUV was gone from the parking lot. I've been looking in every bar and restaurant in the north end. Now I find you in a place like this!"

Ricky slumped into a chair. He was so angry he could barely think. But at the same time finding his brother was such an enormous relief. What if he had left the pub, drunk, and got caught by the police? The judge would throw away the key. Charlie was mumbling some explanation as to why the police would never catch him. Ricky cut him off.

"Come on. We're getting out of here."

"I just ordered another beer. Why don't you have one with me, Ricky? You're too uptight."

"Damned right I'm uptight."

"Remember we used to go drinking all the time? That was great, eh? Why don't we do that anymore?"

Ricky couldn't tell his brother that in the last three years he could barely stand to be in the same room with him. Every time he talked to Charlie he could see that his life was going down the drain, and the more he tried to stop it, the more impossible it became.

"Eh, what happened to us, Ricky?"

"Come on. Let's get out of here. You're coming with me and leaving the car."

"I'm still okay to drive."

"No, you're not. You can't take that chance."

Charlie put his head in his hands. What had come between him and his brother, Ricky? *Must be Leona. She never did like me.* When he looked back up at Ricky, he saw tears gathering in his eyes. "You're upset with me."

"Charlie, you can't keep doing this." Ricky smeared a tear across his cheek with the back of his hand. "You've got to pull yourself together."

"What's a couple of drinks, Ricky?"

"I'll help you. I really will, but you're sliding down, Charlie. It's one bit of trouble after another."

"I'll be okay."

"That's what you always say, and then something else happens. It started back when you broke up with Jennifer."

"Don't bring that up."

"Even before that. But you can't do it anymore. I know I promised Mom, but it's just too much, and you're not doing anything to help yourself."

"What do you want me to do? I work every day."

"I just want you to stay out of trouble. Is that so much to ask?"

"This thing with the girl is just an accident. It's nothing."

"No, it's not! Don't you understand? It's very serious. I don't know what's going to happen when you go back to court, but I know this: If you get picked up for drunk driving tonight, you'll be in jail for a long time."

Just then the waitress arrived with the pint of beer that Charlie had ordered. Ricky looked up at her. "He's not drinking that. Tell me what he owes and I will pay for it."

"I can pay my own tab!" Charlie was suddenly angry at his brother. He was treating him like a child.

"Get your coat. We're getting out of here."

"Don't tell me what to do!"

Ricky rose to his feet. "Get your fucking coat!" They were both almost shouting. People in the bar stopped to listen.

"Leave me alone."

"If you don't leave with me now, we're finished, Charlie." His voice was low and threatening. "You can get your own lawyer. You can get your own car. And you can get yourself another job. Do you understand now, Charlie? Do you understand?"

Ricky took a $50 bill out of his wallet and dropped it on the table. He turned and walked toward the back door of the pub. The waitress rushed to meet him with the bill in her hand.

"The money's on the table," he told her. "His car will stay in the parking lot overnight. We'll get it in the morning."

He looked back. Charlie had his coat and was following him.

CHAPTER 14

It was four in the afternoon on Friday. Mariner was in Sarah Simonac's office, and they were going over the details of the case.

The detective laid it out for her. Copies of the signed witness statements were printed and neatly stapled together. They examined the photos. Mariner showed her the drawing of the intersection that he had created and pointed out how Abbott had turned the corner, how Shelly had slammed into the side of the SUV and fallen under the back right wheel.

He also had a printed list of the criminal convictions of Abbott, including the assault causing bodily harm relating to the break-up of his marriage. Mariner had decided not to show her the police report on the assault. He understood the Crown well enough to believe that it would infuriate her and perhaps cloud her judgement.

After they had gone through the material, Mariner went on to explain the one vulnerable issue in their case. "George Smith—Spider—is, or was, a drug addict."

"Do we really have to use him?"

"If the dangerous driving charge is going to stick, you have to demonstrate that Abbott's driving was out of control. Spider's testimony shows that he drove into the bike lane on at least three occasions as he went along College Street. There was the first shouting match at the stoplight. Then Abbott sped up and cut Spider off by driving into the bike lane. That is dangerous driving right there. When Spider challenged him, he drove up onto the sidewalk and swerved back onto the road. All of this happened before the accident. It adds up to a clear indication that he was driving dangerously. If we don't have Spider's testimony, you won't be able to demonstrate that."

Sarah nodded. Mariner was right. She had to draw out all of these points from Spider's testimony, and once that was done she could make the conclusion that the accident and the death of Shelly McTavish were a consequence of Abbott's dangerous driving.

"But," she asked, "How will this Spider character react when he is cross-examined?"

"I'm worried about that."

"You've met him. What do you think?"

"You know, usually I can predict how a witness will react, but not this time. He's very vulnerable—fragile, almost. He has a history of losing his temper when he is under pressure and getting into trouble. I think he is off the drugs, but it's left him in an anxious state. I've seen it with addicts before."

"The credibility of our witnesses is absolutely vital in this trial."

"Spider's all we've got. Somehow I have confidence in him."

"It could be rough."

"I know."

"I guess you've given me everything I need. I'll read over the witness statements tonight."

The Crown attorney leaned back in her chair. "You know, I really don't like this case. A young woman killed. Every time I see that picture of her with the baby in the newspapers it just—I don't know."

"Breaks your heart."

"Yeah. And then there's the media circus. How can we get a fair trial when everybody in the city has an opinion about it?"

"That's up to the judge."

"I guess, but the media will be listening to every word. It gives an edge to the case."

"I know. It's strange how these things develop. The case has become a symbol of the controversy between cars and bicycles. Those who support Abbott think roads should be only for cars, and those who support bicycles hold up Shelly McTavish as a victim of car culture."

Sarah nodded. Sometimes criminal cases, or any incident, for that matter, take on much broader meanings because they tap into the concerns of the public. "But Shelly wouldn't care about any of that. The truth is that she was just a young mother anxious to get home to her baby."

For a moment, the two of them were lost in thought. Then Sarah leaned forward, propping her elbows on her desk. "Tell me about Abbott." She had come to respect the opinion of this detective.

"He's out of control and has been for some time. He was an accident waiting to happen. He broke up with his wife. He's drinking too much. He is only able to function because he works for his brother, who protects him."

"His lawyer told me the brother is paying for the high-priced legal help."

"I thought so. He's a mess. A danger to himself and Shelly McTavish and anyone else who happens to cross his path."

"What about the wife and the assault causing bodily harm conviction?"

"It's ugly. He beat up his wife. I don't have to paint the picture, but it's not pretty. This man is going downhill fast, and unless he gets a good, hard jolt to bring him to his senses, he will go from one patch of trouble to the next."

Mariner knew he didn't have to describe the assault. Like police, social workers and therapists everywhere, the Crown dealt with cases like this almost every day. They appeared with such regularity that people who worked with them had to erect an emotional barrier to protect themselves or they would be overwhelmed.

"Yeah, well, maybe the court will deliver that jolt to him," she replied.

Mariner nodded. Perhaps that would be the best thing, but it remained a remote possibility.

The meeting broke up. Mariner went back to 52 Division. Sarah read through the witness statements and afterward turned back to the administrative chores that she hated. It was seven o'clock before she got home to her empty condo on the waterfront.

At the very same time Sarah Simonac and Mariner were meeting, James Underhill was discussing the case with Charles, Richard and Leona Abbott in the Bay Street offices of Munro, Stafford and Malone. They were sitting in the corner of his office that held a small table and four comfortable chairs. It was perfect for small meetings.

Underhill had welcomed them, ordered coffee from the receptionist, and they settled into the chairs. The lawyer had the file in front of him, a pad of paper and a pen. He tried to make them feel at ease.

"It is good of you to come in. I am sure that this is difficult for all of you. I will try not to take up too much of your time." Underhill was very good at social chatter. Then he continued by trying to give the context to the discussion.

"I think I should explain that this is a difficult case. I don't mean to alarm you. I think in the end it will be resolved favourably, but the interest of the media and the public in this case gives it special attention, and that can't help but influence the judge."

"Should we ask to have the trial moved?" asked Richard.

"That is a possibility, but I would not recommend it. We have to trust the judge, and I have been told by my colleagues that he is scrupulously fair. The controversy about bicycles in the city is one thing, but we have to ignore that and focus on the events around this alleged offence.

The easy flow of words encouraged Charlie. "Yeah, like, that's right," he said, glancing at his brother and Leona. "Like, it was only an accident."

"Yes, that's true," continued Underhill. "But the unfortunate death of Shelly McTavish has made it rather special. If it was just an accident between a car and a bicycle then we would not have problems but…."

"Then, like, that's the point you've gotta make," interrupted Charlie.

Ricky leaned across and put his hand on his brother's arm. "Let's hear what Mr. Underhill has to say, Charlie. He knows the law."

"Let me tell you what I am going to try to do—my strategy, so to speak. This charge, dangerous driving causing bodily harm, is an indictable offence under the Criminal Code. It is not the most serious offence in the code, but it is very serious. If Charles is convicted, the judge has the option to sentence an offender to up to 14 years in jail and a criminal conviction is registered."

Charlie felt a panic. Fourteen years. He would die in prison. "But…." He was about to interrupt but glanced at his brother and was silent.

Underhill continued. "My strategy is to try to get the charge reduced to careless driving. That is a much less serious charge. It is not a conviction under the Criminal Code; it is under the Ontario Highway Traffic Act. You could lose your licence for a period of time, and the maximum jail sentence is six months."

This time Ricky had to interrupt, "Is there no chance that the charge will be dismissed?"

"I don't believe so. I have carefully read all of the statements of the witnesses. The Crown is obliged to supply them to the defence. And it will be difficult to avoid a conviction. You have admitted to the fact that you were driving the car; that you turned in front of the girl at the intersection; she struck the side of the car; she fell and was run over by the back wheel of your car. We cannot challenge the facts. Our case rests on what is the appropriate charge."

"But it was just an accident," Charlie pleaded. "It could have happened to anyone."

"As a driver, you are responsible for the control of your vehicle. The Crown will argue that you should have seen the girl and avoided her. That will be very hard to dispute. Intent becomes very important. The Crown will try to establish that you intended to hurt her. In my opinion, the best that we can do is to get a reduction of the charge from dangerous driving to careless driving."

Charlie looked desperately at his brother for a moment. Until that moment he had been certain that the high-priced, hot-shot lawyer would find some way to get him off the charge completely. "It was just an accident," he repeated, but this time he sounded much less convincing.

"So what are the possibilities of getting the charge reduced?" Ricky asked.

The coffee had arrived and they continued talking as it was circulated.

"I think, frankly, that is a good possibility, and I wouldn't tell you that if I didn't believe it was true. But there are no guarantees. You have to understand that. It will be up to me to make that case in as convincing a way as possible, and it will be up to the judge to make that decision."

"What about that woman lawyer, the Crown?" asked Charlie.

"She represents the interests of the public. She is important. That certainly is true."

"But they wouldn't send me to jail after I was let out on bail, would they?"

"They might. Bail is another issue completely."

"Holy Christ." Panic caused the word to slip out of Charlie. It was a mistake. He knew that Leona hated swearing. "Sorry about that. Sorry." He was nervous and upset now.

"So let's review the facts here," the lawyer continued. "Mr. Abbott, I sent copies of all of the witness statements to you. Have you read them?"

"Yeah."

"Is there anything in the statements that you dispute or disagree with?"

"Well, there's that stuff about me signalling my turn. I always signal my turns."

"Yes, that's a very important point." Underhill made a note on his pad. "Two of the witnesses say they can't remember, and one says you did not signal the turn. Do you dispute that?"

"Absolutely! I definitely put on my turn signal."

"Okay, good. That's important. I will find a way to get that on the record. Is there anything else?"

"Well, there's all that stuff about me driving in the bicycle lane. That didn't happen."

Again, the lawyer made a note on his pad. "What about the statement of Mr. George Smith, the courier? Did you get into an argument with him?"

"Yeah, but I didn't drive up on the sidewalk."

"So that is not true."

"No. No way." Charlie said it as convincingly as he could.

"Okay, those are important points, but…" and here James Underhill pondered for a moment. He could see that the difficulty he was going to have was how to get these points before the judge. The only one who could claim these things was the accused. "Mr. Abbott," he continued. "How do you feel about testifying before the court?"

"What do you mean?"

"In a criminal trial such as this, the accused is not required to be a witness, but if you choose to testify on your own behalf, you will be subject to cross-examination by the Crown."

"Sure. I'll be a witness," said Charlie. "Then I can set things straight and tell what happened."

"I need to caution you. Cross-examination can be very difficult."

"I can take it."

"Charlie, are you sure?" asked Ricky.

"Course I'm sure."

"But it could mean that the Crown could bring up all sorts of other stuff about your history."

"No," said Underhill. "She can only bring up issues pertinent to the case. After a conviction is registered, then issues like previous driving convictions, work record and so on can be used but not in the trial itself."

"But, Charlie, she's smart and she could tie you up. You don't have to take that chance."

There it was again. Ricky didn't trust him, didn't think he was as smart as he was. He was sick of his brother interfering in his life. He could handle himself. Maybe this would be a way for him to show Ricky once and for all that he could handle himself. "I'm gonna do it. I want to do it. The court needs to hear the truth."

Underhill looked at the two brothers and made a decision. "All right, then, I will put you on the stand, Mr. Abbott. That will make my job easier because I won't have to rely on casting doubt on the other witnesses, but you have to realize that a lot will rest on your testimony."

"I can do it," repeated Charlie. "Once they see that I've got a good job and I am a respectable citizen, they will believe me."

"Well, that's it, then," said the lawyer. "I think we all understand where we are going with this case."

The meeting went on. Underwood explained that if there were a conviction, he would need to have witnesses who could speak to the good character of Charlie.

"I can do that," said Ricky.

"And anyone else?"

Ricky glanced at Leona. "No, I think I'm the best one to do it." He was concerned that if anyone else from the family or the company was put on the stand, the Crown would find a way to make them tell the truth about Charlie—his drinking, what happened when his family broke up, his work record before he was employed at the refrigerator company. There was a lot to hide, and if the truth had to be bent, it was better that he did it.

Underhill tore off the page from his writing pad and put it into the file. "All right, then, I will see you in court tomorrow morning at 10."

Leona had said nothing during the meeting. They drove Charlie to his apartment building, and then the two of them continued on to their house in Don Mills. She felt she had to say something, but she felt uneasy. She knew that her husband did not like criticisms of his brother.

"I've got a bad feeling about this trial," she said as they drove through the suburbs in their darkened car.

"What's that?" Ricky had asked her to come to the meeting with the lawyer because he valued her opinion. She was central to his family life, but he saw his brother as his responsibility.

"Things have been building up. First there were the driving infractions, the drinking, and then the assault on Jennifer. Now he kills this girl in the accident. He's unrealistic and defensive, scared. You could see it in the meeting."

"What could I do? He insisted on testifying."

"It's not just that I'm worried about. Once they register a conviction either for dangerous driving or careless driving, then everything is going to come out. You have to think about how it will reflect on you and on the company and the family. Think of his kids. They are going to learn about it."

Ricky felt sick. Whenever there was stress around the family, he went into emotional turmoil that made him feel physically ill. Over the last two days it was worse than ever. "But what can I do?" He was pleading for an answer.

"I don't know."

"Charlie has always been a problem. He's my younger brother, and he could never do anything right. I went on to university and became an engineer, and Charlie couldn't get out of Grade 10. He went from job to job. His marriage was a mess. I've tried to look after him, but look where it's got me."

"Maybe you should cut him loose. Let him get his own job, find his own way. Maybe you're not doing him a favour by looking after him every time he gets into trouble."

"But he's my brother. I promised Mom that I'd look after him. We all knew he was a problem. But now, Charlie up on the witness stand.... He's going to make a mess of it. But what can I do?"

He glanced at his wife sitting beside him in the reflected glow from the lights on the dashboard. He was a brilliant engineer who could solve complex technical problems, but this was a problem that was beyond him.

"I don't know, Ricky, but it's coming to a head. Something is going to change."

CHAPTER 15

At 10 in the morning the doors to the courtroom were opened and the public moved inside. Several members of the press were in attendance. A number of spectators who had followed the case filled the benches. The subpoenaed witnesses sat among them.

James Underhill went to stand beside the table reserved for the defence on the other side of the bar of the courtroom. He motioned for Charles Abbott, the accused, to come and sit beside him. Behind them, on the other side of the bar, sat Richard and Leona Abbott.

Sarah Simonac was one of the last to come into the courtroom. She carried files and papers relating to the case. She paused for a moment to talk to Mariner and his partner, Alex, who had positioned themselves behind the Crown's table on the other side of the bar.

The clerk and stenographer took their places. A courtroom guard in uniform stood beside the dock. People chatted until the clerk stood and announced in a loud voice, "All rise!" Everyone got to their feet. The judge, wearing his black robe, came into the courtroom through a door at the back. "Judge Norman Taylor presiding." The judge took his seat and in unison everyone in the courtroom sat down. The trial of Charles Abbott had begun.

The accused was asked to stand, and the charge was read by the clerk. "That you are accused of driving dangerously causing bodily harm. How do you plead, guilty or not guilty?"

"Not guilty."

Detective Mariner was the first in the witness box. The Crown led him through the evidence. The accident was described. Mariner showed the drawing of the intersection and pointed out how Abbott had turned the corner, the victim had hit the side of the SUV, had fallen and was crushed under the car. The photos were shown to the two lawyers and the judge, but they were not shown to the public. If asked, the judge would have ruled that the photos were too graphic.

At the conclusion of Mariner's testimony, the Crown asked, "Did Mr. Charles Abbott admit to driving the car that killed Shelly McTavish?"

"Yes."

"Was Mr. Abbott co-operative?"

"At first he refused to take the breathalyzer, but when we explained his rights to him and the consequences of not taking the test, he agreed."

"Thank you, Detective Mariner."

In the cross-examination James Underhill, the defence lawyer, made only one point. "Detective, would you tell us again what Mr. Abbott registered on the breathalyzer?"

"The reading was .03."

"So according to accepted standards, he was not intoxicated."

"That is correct."

"Thank you."

Next, Alex was put on the stand, and he corroborated the evidence already given. There were no further questions.

Then the three eyewitnesses to the accident gave their testimony. Each of them described the same sequence of events. They had witnessed the arguments between the courier and the driver of the SUV, who they now knew was Charles Abbott. The first shouting match had happened at the light. Then Abbott blocked the bicycle lane with his car, and a second argument happened between the courier and the driver. The SUV then drove up onto the sidewalk and lurched back onto the road. The SUV came up to the light at Dovercourt. Shelly McTavish was peddling hard to make the light while it was still green. All three said that the car cut right in front of her, and she did not have a chance to avoid the collision.

The Crown asked each of them if the accused had driven into the bicycle lane before the accident. One said he did not notice. The other two said he had crowded the lane but they could not be certain if the car had actually come into the bicycle lane.

Then all three were asked the same question by the Crown. "Did the driver of the SUV put on his right directional signal to indicate his turn?"

The first two said they could not remember. The third, Joel Alexander, was very clear. "No, he did not put on his indicator. I would have seen the flashing light."

In the cross-examination, the defence tried to challenge that claim. "Mr. Alexander, how can you be certain that the directional signal was not put on?"

"I would have seen it. I was riding two or three lengths behind Ms. McTavish. I could see everything."

"But the other two witnesses didn't see it."

"They said they don't remember seeing it," Alexander corrected the lawyer. "I remember perfectly. No signal was given. The rider didn't have a chance."

"What do you think of people who ride in cars?"

"I ride in cars all the time. I'm no purist. I even have my driver's licence. I'm not inventing this because I don't like cars, if that's what you're implying. He didn't put on his signal, and that's the truth."

Underhill gave up. The testimony was damaging, but he was not going to break this witness down.

The next witness called was George Smith. Spider was sitting beside his girlfriend, Jay, anxiously anticipating this moment. Ever since he had come into the courtroom, he had practised deep breathing to try to keep control. His hands were shaking and he was perspiring. The courtroom reminded him of all the times that he had been up on charges.

When his name was called, Jay squeezed his hand for encouragement. He got to his feet and walked to the witness box. Spider was wearing his best pants and shirt, but the shirt did not hide the tattoo creeping up his neck or reappearing on his right hand. Looking around at all of the others in the courtroom, he knew he should have worn a suit and tie, but he didn't have one.

He was asked if he would "Tell the truth, the whole truth, so help you God?"

"Yes," he replied, but his mouth was dry and the word was barely audible. "Yes," he repeated for everyone to hear.

Mariner concentrated on every word of the testimony. This was the key witness in the case. Sarah

Simonac, had Spider's statement in her hand and she led him through it, getting him to repeat in his own words what he had witnessed. This was familiar ground for Spider, and he gained confidence as he related the events.

"Tell me, Mr. Smith, why did you challenge Mr. Abbott at the stoplight?"

"His car kept coming into the bike lane. I was afraid he was going to hit someone."

"Did anyone else get hit by his car?"

"No, but there were a lot of cyclists out on the street. Like, I don't think people in cars understand how, you know, how dangerous it can be ridin' a bike. Like, you don't stand a chance up against a piece of metal, if you know what I mean. So I thought I needed to tell him to be careful. That's what I was tryin' to do."

"So there was the first confrontation was at the stoplight. Then what happened?"

"I left. I went through the light, and I was ridin' along the bike path, and suddenly he cut me off. His car came right into the bike lane, and I had to slam on my brakes or I would have hit him."

"Did that frighten you?"

"Yeah, I mean that's a big car. He could have killed me. I didn't do nothin' to him. I just wanted to talk to him, but then, like, he drove right at me."

"What happened then?"

"I guess I was a little steamed, and I put my bike up against a tree or parking meter, and … and we exchanged some words."

"Were you angry?"

"Yeah, I shouted at him. I told him to be careful. That he could hurt someone. That he shouldn't drive in the bike lane. Things like that."

"Did he say anything in return?"

"He was mad. He said, 'Roads were for cars, not bicycles.' Things like that. He was angry. I could see that. His face was all red. And he swore at me."

"Did you shout back at him?"

"Yeah, but I didn't swear at him. Like, I wasn't gonna hit him or nothing like that. I was just tryin' to make him understand that he was driving dangerously."

"Then what happened?"

"I'd put my bike up against this lamppost, and I walked around to the driver's side, and I shouted at him again, trying to make him understand. Then I got a real good look at him, and I could see he was panicked or scared or somethin'. Then he stepped on the accelerator, and his car drove up on the sidewalk, then swerved back out onto the road and went up the street."

"Do you think he was frightened about what you might do?"

"Yeah, I think so. He panicked. But I wasn't gonna do nothin' to him. All I was gonna do was to tell him to be more careful."

"What did you do next?"

"I left. I got out of there. I went across the street, and I went up to Dovercourt and I turned left. I didn't want anything to do with this guy."

"So you did not witness the accident."

"No."

"Thank you, Mr. Smith. I don't have any more questions."

Sarah Simonac sat down and the defence lawyer got to his feet. Spider knew this was where trouble would start. He remembered what Mariner had said to him. "Just tell the truth, Spider. All you have to do is tell the truth." He breathed deeply to calm his nerves.

James Underhill approached the witness with a file in his hand that he was reading intently. Then he lowered it and looked at Spider. His handsome looks and well-made suit projected the look of authority.

He began with an odd question. "Mr. Smith, what do your friends call you?"

"Spider. They call me Spider." He knew immediately what Underhill was doing.

"Spider." That's interesting. How did you get a name like that?"

He felt his skin crawl. His hands shook. "I've been called that since I was a kid." His voice was almost a whisper.

"What's that? Speak up please so everyone can hear you," Underhill demanded. He was in command. Dominating.

"I've been called that since I was a child, sir."

Mariner leaned forward. Underhill was using an old courtroom tactic to frighten and intimidate the witness. It was designed to get under the skin of the vulnerable and make them lose their nerve, and it often worked.

"Spider. I see." The lawyer's voice was loud, demanding. "You work as a bike courier, Spider. Is that correct?"

"Yes."

"Speak up, please. Now tell me, Mr. Spider, have you ever been convicted of a crime?"

It was cold fear that went through Spider's body. Everything about his past was going to come out now.

"Your Honour, that question is not relevant to this trial." It was Sarah Simonac

"Your Honour, I am trying to determine the credibility of this witness," replied Underhill.

"I will allow this question, but I will not allow any follow-up questions in this area, Mr. Underhill."

"Thank you." He turned back to the witness. "Spider, I am going to repeat my question. Have you ever been convicted of a crime?"

"Yes." Spider said firmly and then waited for the next question. "Tell the truth" was what Mariner had said.

There were many more questions, and with each one Spider listened carefully and tried to answer as precisely and as honestly as he could. There were questions about Abbott driving into the bicycle lane, and Spider explained that he saw it happen three times before he confronted him at the stoplight. He was asked if he was angry. Yes, he was upset, he admitted.

"You claim that the accused cut you off with his vehicle. You put down your bike, you walked around to the driver's side of the vehicle and shouted at Mr. Abbott. Were you going to assault him, Spider?"

"No, definitely not. I said that before. I was just trying to tell him to be more careful," answered Spider confidently.

"Then after the accused drove away, why did you get on your bicycle and speed away? Were you afraid that you might be arrested for assault or threatening?"

"No! I could see that he was out of control. I thought maybe he was drunk or that maybe something was wrong with him and that someone could get hurt." Spider was speaking clearly now. "And that is exactly what happened. His face was pink. He was angry at me. I could see that. So as he drove up toward the light, he could see a cyclist coming along beside him in the mirror, and he thought it was me, and when he got to the corner he turned right in front of the cyclist. He was trying to hurt me, but the cyclist wasn't me. It was Shelly McTavish."

James Underhill was suddenly panicked. Spider had sketched out a scenario where his client had purposely set out to injure a cyclist. If that stayed in the judge's mind, Abbott was sunk. "What evidence do you have to make such a claim?" he demanded sharply.

"I saw how frightened or mad he was. Like, when I went to challenge him, he drove up over the curb and the sidewalk and back onto the road. He was panicked. I could see it in his face, and I've seen that lots of times in people. He was so angry that he wanted to get back at me and that's why the girl got killed."

"This is nothing but wild speculation. How can you attribute this motivation to him?"

"I know what I know!" Spider had no respect for this lawyer now. He was trying to cover up for his client. "Abbott was out of control. His face was red. He was frightened. He'd lost it. He was angry at me. He thought he saw me coming and so he turned quickly at the corner, so quick that no bike rider could stop in time. He was trying to get me—injure me. Only it wasn't me. It was this girl, this mother, Shelly McTavish. I am just sorry I didn't stay around because maybe I could have done somethin' to save this woman."

Spider was confident and sure of himself, and now it was Underhill who was in a panic. He spoke directly to the judge. "Your Honour, you have to discount what this witness is saying. He has no qualifications to make judgements such as this. It is all mere speculation."

"Thank you, Mr. Underhill. Do you have any more questions for the witness?"

"No, Your Honour."

"You can step down, Mr. Smith." We will take a 15-minute break." Everyone stood as the judge left the courtroom.

Spider was partway back to his seat when Mariner met him. Jay joined them and took his hand.

"Spider, I want you to know this," Mariner began. "I'm proud of you. You told the truth and didn't back away. I know it was very difficult, but you stood up for what's right. You are a powerful and honourable man, Spider. Thank you." Then he touched his arm and smiled.

Tears were rolling down Spider's face as the detective walked away. This was the first time in his life that someone had praised him in that way. It gave him hope for a better future.

When Spider went out into the hallway he was met with a crush of media. Video cameras rolled; cameras flashed; questions were shouted. Like a seasoned politician, Spider delivered a simple message. "Streets are for everyone, and they must be made safe for cyclists."

CHAPTER 16

After the recess, the defence put Charles Abbott on the witness stand. He took the oath to tell the truth, and then, because he was a defence witness, the questioning was begun by James Underhill.

"Mr. Abbott, tell us in your own words what happened the night Shelly McTavish died."

"It was after work on a Friday night, and so I went for a drive. I wunderas coming along College Street, and I got to the light at Dovercourt, and I turned right. There was a bump on the side of my car, and then it felt like I drove over something so I stopped and got out. She was lying there. It was an accident."

"So you are saying you did not drive dangerously. It was an accident. Do you think the accident could have been prevented?"

"Well, yeah, if she had seen my directional signal, she would have known I was turning right and would have stopped. Maybe she was going too fast. I don't know."

"Mr. Abbott, one of the witnesses testified that you did not put on your direction signal. Two others said they could not remember. Explain what happened."

"I did put on my signal."

"This is an important point. You are saying you signalled your turn?"

"Yes. I always signal my turns."

"Leaving aside the directional signal, did you take the corner carefully, Mr. Abbott? Was it hurried? Did you turn dangerously, anything like that?"

"No, it was just an ordinary turn."

"Did you give enough time in your turn for a cyclist to stop?"

"Yes. She must have been coming too fast."

"All right. Thank you. Now, Mr. George Smith, or Spider as he calls himself, testified that there was an altercation between the two of you on College Street. Do you remember that?"

"Yes."

"Tell me about it."

"Well, I stopped at the red light, the one before Dovercourt, and he came up beside me on his bike, and he started shouting at me. So I rolled down my window and was going to ask him what he had said, but he took off on his bike. So I drove up and caught up with him."

"What were you going to do?"

"I wanted to talk to him."

"Did you talk?"

"No, because he started shouting at me. He put his bicycle against a tree or somethin' and he came around to the driver's side, and he shouted at me again."

"Do you remember what he said?"

"Something about driving in the cycling lane."

"Did you drive in the bicycle lane?"

"No. Well, I did when I drove up to talk to this guy, but not before that."

"So did you shout back at Spider?"

"I might have a little. I don't know."

"Then what happened?"

"I left. I drove away."

"And shortly after there was the accident."

"Yes."

"Do you think the shouting match with Mr. Smith had anything to do with the accident?"

"No."

"So in your opinion, Mr. Abbott, this was an ordinary accident and unfortunately Ms. McTavish was killed."

"Yes."

"That is why you have pleaded not guilty to the dangerous driving causing bodily harm charge."

"Yes."

"Thank you." Underhill walked back to his seat and gave a nod to Sarah Simonac to indicate that it was her turn to cross-examine the witness. The Crown got to her feet and walked slowly toward the witness box. She held no file or note in her hands.

"So, Mr. Abbott, you were just out for a drive on a Friday night. Is that right?"

"Yes."

"Why didn't you go home?"

"I live alone. I wanted to go out. It was a Friday night."

"You wanted some action. Is that right?"

"Well, yeah, I mean, I was looking for somethin' to do."

"So you were out cruising the streets in your big SUV. Who owns that vehicle, Mr. Abbott?"

"The company."

"What company?"

"My brother's refrigerator company."

"So you work for your brother."

"Yes. I'm a salesman, and I need a car for work."

"Do you have permission to cruise around in the company car after work?"

"Yeah. It's my car. I can use it for anything."

"Do you cruise around often?"

"I guess. Yeah."

"So you were just driving around the city looking for something to do, and you happened to come along College Street."

"Yeah. I wasn't planning it or anything like that."

"So George Smith and the other three witnesses testified that you were driving erratically as you came along College Street. They all said you crowded the lane and Smith said you came into the bicycle lane on more than one occasion."

"That's not true."

"Do you deny that you drove into the bicycle lane?"

"Yeah."

"Was it possible that you might have drifted into the bicycle lane and didn't know it? There is no barrier between the bike lane and the street."

"No, I didn't go into the bike lane at all."

"Then you are you telling me Mr. Smith is a liar?"

"Well, just look at him. He's, like, a bicycle courier."

"Are you saying all bicycle couriers are liars?"

"No."

"Then you don't like bicycle couriers."

"It's not that."

"You don't like the way Mr. Smith looks?" The questions were coming fast now.

"Yeah, maybe somethin' like that." Abbott was starting to feel agitated, annoyed.

"You think they should dress better?"

"Well, they're rough. Like, you heard him say that he had a criminal record."

"So if you didn't drive into the bike lane, why did Mr. Smith shout at you?"

"I don't know."

"Don't you think it's pretty unusual that someone would get into a shouting match with you if nothing had happened?"

Charlie was sweating now. "I don't know."

"You don't know?" She looked at him for a long moment. "Unusual?"

The Crown backed away a step and then turned. "Do you have a criminal record, Mr. Abbott?"

Underhill was on his feet. "Your Honour, the record of an accused is not allowed to be revealed in a trial until after a conviction is determined."

"Your Honour," the Crown replied. "You required Mr. Smith to reveal that he had a criminal record. That was done so that the court could evaluate the credibility of the witness. Mr. Abbott has chosen to be a witness in his trial, and it is only fair that he be required to answer the same question so we can judge his credibility."

"All right, I will allow it," the judge said. "But I do not want any further questions in this area."

"I will repeat my question, Mr. Abbott," the Crown continued. "Do you have a criminal record?"

"Yes." He felt trapped. He knew his brother, Ricky, would not like his record revealed.

She continued with rapid-fire questions. "So you think that Mr. Smith is rough. That was your word. When you saw him the evening of the accident, did you think he was a criminal?"

"I don't know."

"Were you frightened of him?"

"No."

"Not even a little? You say Smith was rough. He had his courier bag over his shoulder, and you don't like couriers. Are you sure you weren't frightened of him?"

"No, not at all."

"It's easy to understand why you might be frightened. He is lean and tall. He is a lot younger than you and in much better shape. How did you feel when he shouted at you?"

"Upset, I guess. Maybe I was scared a little."

"But you just said you weren't frightened. And you told Mr. Underhill you were not frightened. Now you say you were scared. What's the truth?"

"I don't know. I guess I was scared a little. Like, he's scary, you know, tattoos and everything."

"So let's get this straight. Your first words were exchanged at the stoplight. Then Smith took off on his bike. You sped ahead and caught up with him. You drove into the bike lane and cut him off."

"I didn't go into the bike lane."

"Excuse me. You admitted to Mr. Underhill that you did drive into the bike lane to block Smith. Now you are saying that is not true? What is the truth?"

"Yeah, well maybe I did go in a little." Charlie wasn't sure exactly what he had said.

"So now you are admitting you went into the bicycle lane with your car. What is the truth, Mr. Abbott?"

He was confused, afraid to say anything in case it just gave her more ammunition. She waited, but Charlie could say nothing. The Crown continued in a loud, commanding voice.

"Smith admitted that he was upset because you drove into the bike lane and almost hit him. You blocked the bike lane with your car. You were sitting in your big car, and he was vulnerable on his bike. So it is not surprising that he was angry. Isn't that right?"

"I could see it on his face."

"And that must have made you panic. He was young and fit. You don't like couriers. You thought he was a criminal. He was angry at you. Then he came around to the driver's side of the car. He shouted at you. That must have scared you."

"He was comin' for me."

"So you floored the accelerator. Right?"

"Like, I didn't know what might happen."

"You were scared. You had to get out of there. Is that right?"

"Yeah…."

"You lost control of your car. It lurched up over the curb and onto the sidewalk, and then back onto the road again. You had to get away from this guy before he got you. Right?"

"I always had control of the car."

"No, you were driving out of control. Your car went up on the sidewalk. You were panicked. People in control of their car don't drive on the sidewalk. You were driving dangerously."

"No!"

"Yes!" She waited for a moment and then continued. "I can understand why you lost control. We've all felt panic before. You were upset. Who was this courier anyway? You were a businessman. He was nothing but a courier. Then the cars up ahead started moving through the light, and you followed them at their speed."

"Yeah."

"You must have looked in your rear-view mirror to see if the courier was chasing you. It would be the natural thing to do."

"Yeah, I saw him."

"And he was riding along almost beside you as you were moving up toward the stoplight at Dovercourt. Isn't that right?"

"Yes," he said in a weak voice.

"You watched him come in your rear-view mirror attached to the right-hand side of your car. You were angry at him. You wanted to teach him a lesson. You watched him come in the rear-view mirror, and the two of you got to the corner at almost the same time. Maybe you were just a little ahead of him. Right?"

"Yeah."

"And just then you turned the corner hard and quick. Isn't that right?"

She waited for him to say something, but he was immobilized, staring at the floor, as if at that moment her description took him back to that fateful second. "Why did you turn the corner, Mr. Abbott?"

"It was an accident," he said softly.

"Did you turn on your directional signal before you turned right?"

"Yes."

"Are you calling Joel Alexander a liar?"

"He wasn't there."

"Yes, he was. He was two or three lengths behind Shelly McTavish. That is his testimony. He said he saw everything."

She waited until it was clear he could not reply. "Did you look to see if anyone was in the bike lane before you made your turn?"

Words would not come. Charlie stared at her for the longest time. The courtroom was completely hushed as everyone waited for an answer, but none came.

She took a step back as if to break the spell. "I don't think you signalled your turn, Mr. Abbott. You were angry and scared—maybe ashamed at what had happened, and you wanted to get back at the courier and teach him a lesson. You drove up to the Dovercourt light watching the cyclist in your rear-view mirror. You admitted that. You thought it was the courier. You wanted to get back at him, so you turned your SUV right in front of him. I don't know if you intended to kill Mr. Smith. Maybe you just wanted to frighten him. But the consequences were fatal. Only it wasn't the courier at all. It was the unfortunate Shelly McTavish."

Sweat had drenched Charlie's clothes. The courtroom was completely quiet. Charlie tried to understand what was happening, but he wasn't sure anymore. He wasn't sure of anything.

Then someone was speaking. It was the judge. "Do you have any more questions, Ms. Simonac?"

"No further questions, Your Honour."

"Thank you, Ms. Simonac. Mr. Abbott, you may step down. We will break for lunch and resume at 2 p.m. We will hear the closing statements at that time."

CHAPTER 17

Judge Norman Taylor asked the clerk to get him an egg salad sandwich and a juice for lunch. He had learned that taking time to reflect on a case right after hearing the testimony helped him to sort out what was important. When his sandwich came, he sat behind his desk and tried to think about the Abbott case.

There was always a lot of irrelevant crap that came out in a trial. "A criminal trial is not the Supreme Court of Canada," one of his fellow judges was fond of saying. At that level only the lawyers talked. All that was debated were the legal arguments. In a criminal case like this, emotions and misperceptions clouded everything, and the judge had to clear all the crap away to get at what was really important and find the truth.

Judge Taylor knew from the beginning that the key question in the Abbott case was the degree of recklessness of the driving. There were three options in the final outcome: dangerous driving, careless driving and acquittal. An acquittal was out of the question. There would be a huge public outcry if that was the verdict, and the evidence of reckless driving was far too strong to ignore.

Careless driving had not been mentioned in the trial, but the judge knew that this would be the argument that the defence lawyer would mount in his summation. It was the only defence that was available, after all. Underhill would argue that although there was some level of negligence in the driving of Abbott, it was not dangerous driving, and therefore deserved the lesser charge of careless driving.

The differences in the two charges were quite significant. Dangerous driving was a charge in the Criminal Code with a maximum sentence of 14 years. Careless driving was not a criminal offence. It was in the Ontario Highway Traffic Act, and the maximum sentence was the suspension of the driver's licence and up to six months in jail.

Those were the choices, and it was up to him to decide what was the appropriate charge and sentence. The degree of recklessness or neglect was the key element. The strongest bit of evidence came out in the cross-examination when Abbott admitted he watched the bicycle in his rear-view mirror as he drove up to the Dovercourt light. He turned the corner quickly, knowing full well that a cyclist was right beside him. If that wasn't dangerous driving then what was?

There were other examples. Smith testified that Abbott's SUV had come into the bicycle lane along College Street a number of times. It was denied by the accused, but it was hard to believe. Abbott was hardly a credible witness. The Crown had demolished him. More important, even Abbott admitted that he drove into the bike lane to cut off Smith and then drove up onto the sidewalk. Again, that's dangerous driving.

Still, what was the appropriate charge? He just wasn't sure. Maybe he would have to wait to hear the final arguments of the lawyers. It was while he was turning this over in his mind that another thought occurred to him.

Abbott obviously had deep pockets. His lawyer, James Underhill, was from a top corporate law firm on Bay Street. That meant cost was no barrier to justice. If the dangerous driving conviction was registered, it was likely it would be appealed.

A good lawyer could always dream up grounds for appeal, and there were some in this case. There was the decision he had made to require Abbott to reveal he had a criminal record. The judge could almost write out the grounds for that appeal in his head: "This decision was prejudicial to the accused, Charles Abbott, because it implied that he was a habitual criminal." No doubt that would be taken seriously by the higher court because disclosure of a criminal record before conviction was a violation of well-established precedent.

Another issue had to do with the way the testimony was handled. Was Simonac, the Crown, too aggressive in her cross examination of Abbott? Judge Taylor liked to allow a free-wheeling cross-examination because he found that's how issues came to light. What was surprising was that the defence, Underhill, did not object to try to save his client. It showed his lack of experience in criminal trials. It was unlikely that an appeal court would look at that issue but he couldn't be sure.

Finally, perhaps the strongest ground for appeal was the intense interest of the public in the case. The defence could argue that the accused was not given a fair trial and never could have received one in Toronto because of the notoriety of the case. The trial should have been moved to another venue.

Judge Taylor didn't like any of this. No judge liked to have his cases appealed, because the implication was that he did not handle the case properly. The appeal court was usually careful not to directly criticize a judge, and its decisions were written in legalistic language that only lawyers could understand, but all judges were part of the legal community. They knew when criticism was justified.

Then there was the publicity of this particular case that he had to think about. "Not only must justice be done; justice must be seen to be done." That was the rule drummed into every young lawyer. He knew that the media would give the case and his decision prominent play the next day. Their coverage would determine what the public thought about the case. That was the biggest worry of all.

It was all a bit of a juggling act. How could a judge make fair and objective decisions in high-profile cases like this? The public believed that justice must be imposed in a completely impartial way, but only if they agreed with the sentence. Added to this, the judge making the decision was all too human, with prejudices and blind spots. Justice is impossible, completely impossible, he concluded. But still he had to go into that courtroom and make a decision.

At two o'clock the doors to the courtroom were opened; the media, spectators and witnesses came inside and settled onto the benches. The Crown took her place and the defence attorney sat at the table beside the accused. Detective Mariner sat behind Sarah Simonac. Alex had gone back to the station. The Abbott family positioned themselves behind the defence table. The clerk, stenographer and guard took their places. When everything was readied, the clerk stood up. "All rise," she called. The assembly rose. Judge Norman Taylor entered and sat in his chair. The spectators sat again. The trial was ready to resume.

"Mr. Underhill, do you have any more witnesses you wish to present?" asked the judge.

"No, Your Honour."

"Ms. Simonac?"

"No, Your Honour."

"Are you ready for your final summations?"

Both indicated they were ready. As was the tradition, the Crown would give her summation first. Sarah Simonac got to her feet and addressed the court.

"Thank you, Your Honour. This has been an emotional trial and a difficult one for everyone involved. A young mother was killed on our city streets by a car, a powerful SUV. That has sparked a controversy in the media among politicians and the public as to who is responsible for this tragic accident. The core of that controversy is, should the city devise more effective ways to make the streets safe for cyclists, but that is not the concern of this court. We are here to determine the degree of responsibility of the accused, Mr. Charles Abbott, in the death of Ms. Shelly McTavish.

"It is my belief that the evidence that has come out in this trial show that Mr. Abbott should be found guilty of the charge of dangerous driving causing bodily harm. Let me review the facts.

"On the evening in question Mr. Abbott was driving west on College Street. Mr. George Smith has testified that the SUV that Mr. Abbott was driving came into the bicycle lane on at least three occasions as he was driving west. This was corroborated by the other three witnesses, who said that Abbott's car crowded the bike lane, but the accused claims this is not true. I find it hard to believe Mr. Abbott for two reasons. If he had not driven into the bike lane, there would have been no reason for Mr. Smith to confront him at the stoplight. Second, erratic driving by Mr. Abbott was a pattern that happened at other times that evening.

"The arguments between Mr. Smith and Mr. Abbott were in two stages. At the stoplight, Mr. Smith, who was riding his bicycle, shouted at Abbott, who was sitting in his car. Smith then rode through the light. Once the light changed Abbott chased after him and cut him off by positioning his car across the bike lane. Again, words were exchanged, and I believe the cross-examination of Mr. Abbott demonstrated that he was frightened. He drove up over the curb and the sidewalk and back onto the road. That is an indication of panic.

"Smith left shortly after that confrontation, but Abbott continued driving west toward the Dovercourt light. He has admitted that he watched a cyclist in the rear-view mirror attached to the right side of the car. He watched carefully. At the light the cyclist was almost beside his vehicle, and then he abruptly turned the corner at the light, right in front of her. So abruptly that she did not have the chance to stop. She hit the side of the car, fell and the back wheel rolled over her. There is some question whether Mr. Abbott used his turning signal. One witness said clearly that he did not, but the accused claims he did. Frankly, I don't believe Abbott. If he had given adequate indication that he was turning by signalling, then Ms. McTavish and others could have stopped in time. As we heard from the witnesses, they all had a hard time coming to a stop in time.

"There is the important question of intent. Did Mr. Abbott intend to injure the cyclist or was it simply an accident? He admitted that he was angry after the confrontation with Mr. Smith. He admitted he watched the cyclist in his rear-view mirror as he or she approached the Dovercourt light. And we know that he turned very quickly and unexpectedly. The cyclist did not have a chance to avoid the car. I believe there is enough evidence to conclude that Abbott intended to injure the cyclist. It was not a premeditated act, but his anger made him act impulsively, and that led to the cyclist's death. That cyclist was not Mr. Smith, the courier; it was the unfortunate Ms. Shelly McTavish.

"Those are the facts, Your Honour, and I believe there is ample evidence to convict Charles Abbott of the charge of dangerous driving causing bodily harm."

Sarah Simonac had finished talking. The courtroom was completely hushed as she took her seat.

"Thank you, Ms. Simonac," the judge said. "Mr. Underhill, if you please."

The lawyer for the defence got to his feet. He had come into this case thinking his adversaries were weak, second- or third-tier policemen and legal counsel, but now he understood he had seriously underestimated his opposition. It would be difficult to refute the arguments of the Crown.

"Your Honour, the Crown believes that the charge of dangerous driving causing bodily harm is the appropriate charge in this case. I, however, disagree. I believe careless driving is a much more appropriate. Let me give my reasons.

"Ms. Simonac has placed great weight on the evidence that Mr. Abbott drove into the bike lane on College Street on several occasions, but let's look at the evidence. It was given by Mr. George Smith, hardly a credible witness. Other witnesses said that he crowded the bike lane, but, when questioned, they could not say for sure if the wheels of Mr. Abbott's vehicle crossed the white line separating the bicycle lane. I am sure the police made a thorough investigation in this case, but they did not come up with any other witnesses that could corroborate this claim. I think that is significant. I believe that this evidence must be discounted.

"Second, I agree that there was an altercation between Mr. Smith and Mr. Abbott—an argument, a shouting match, call it what you will. Certainly a disagreement broke out between these two men. But what is unusual about an argument? It happens every day. Yes, Mr. Abbott drove into the bicycle lane in the second of these confrontations. Yes, he should not have done that, but it hardly constitutes dangerous driving. Careless driving, yes; dangerous driving, no.

"Now, the third incident is what happened as Mr. Abbott approached the Dovercourt stoplight. I have to admit that I found the description of this event by Ms. Simonac nothing but wild speculation. We know where she got this idea. It was first suggested by Mr. Smith, Spider, as he calls himself. He claimed that the accused was watching the cyclist approach in the rear-view mirror. This is nothing but speculation. Mr. Smith was not even there and Ms. Simonac was not there either.

"Your Honour, in our legal system we give the accused the benefit of the doubt. Guilt must be established beyond a shadow of a doubt. In my opinion, there is a great deal of doubt in many different elements of this case. A finding of dangerous driving causing bodily harm is not appropriate. The only sensible decision in this case is careless driving."

Underhill had finished and walked toward the defence table.

"Thank you, Mr. Underhill..." the judge began.

"Your Honour," the Crown interrupted. "I am compelled to comment on the gross inaccuracy of Mr. Underhill's remarks."

"Yes?"

"He claimed that the scenario I sketched out, that Mr. Abbott watched the figure of the cyclist in his rear-view mirror as he approached the stoplight, as wild speculation. Your Honour, Mr. Abbott admitted under oath that he watched the figure in his rear-view mirror. It was not my invention. The accused admitted it!"

"Mr. Underhill?"

"He might have seen a figure, but he didn't plot to kill that person."

"No one has claimed Mr. Abbott plotted to kill anyone. I called it an impulsive act, but there was intent. This I do know. The actions of Mr. Abbott leading up to the death of Shelly McTavish show gross neglect and sustain the charge of dangerous driving causing bodily harm."

"How can you say this?" replied Underhill. He knew he had to refute this claim or the case was lost.

"Thank you! Thank you!" Judge Norman Taylor interrupted. He hated lawyers engaging in heated exchanges in his courtroom.

Both lawyers glared at each other as they returned to their seats.

The judge shuffled his papers and tried to collect his thoughts. He was tempted to remand the case for one week and then give sentence, but that would annoy virtually everyone, especially the press. Anyway, he had already made up his mind. What was the point in waiting? He began slowly, marshalling his thoughts as he spoke.

"I would like to thank everyone involved in this case. Whenever a young person is needlessly killed it evokes strong emotions. In particular, I would like to thank the witnesses. You gave your testimony in an open and frank way. Courts could not function without the involvement of citizens committed to telling the truth.

"The arguments on both sides in this case have been spirited and well considered. The case hinges on a judgement call as to whether Mr. Abbott drove in a dangerous or careless manner. Through the witnesses, the cross-examinations and the summaries of councils, I am convinced that the truth has come out as much as is humanly possible. Would the accused please stand up?"

James Underhill looked at his client and nodded. Both of them stood.

"Mr. Abbott, I am finding you guilty of careless driving." There was an audible gasp from the spectators. Judge Taylor continued as if he had not heard it. "I am sentencing you to six months in jail and a loss of your driver's licence for five years."

The judge folded up his papers and got to his feet. "All rise," said the clerk and the judge exited the courtroom.

The court guard put his hand on the arm of Charles Abbott. "Come with me, sir."

"Six months?" said Charles Abbott, shocked and confused. He turned to look at his brother. Ricky was standing ramrod straight. Leona held onto his arm and whispered into his ear, but he did not hear.

"We beat the dangerous driving charge," said Underhill, feeling the flush of victory.

"Then why am I going to jail?" asked Charlie, but there was no answer. He was being escorted away to the holding cells by the guard.

Sarah Simonac paused beside Mariner on her way out of the courtroom. "Fucking bastard," she muttered intently so only he would hear. "The judge didn't have the guts to convict him of dangerous driving. We had him dead to rights."

CHAPTER 18

At about four that afternoon Mariner received a phone call from Sarah Simonac. "Look, I'm sorry I rushed out after the trial. Would you like to have dinner tonight to discuss what happened?"

"That would be nice." Mariner like the directness of the offer, but it was only over dinner that he got the sense of what it was all about.

They met in the Peter Pan Restaurant on Queen Street West, a quiet place they both felt comfortable with. They were semi-public figures in Toronto legal circles, and it was good to be discreet.

Over a bottle of wine, and before the meal came, they dispensed with the unfinished business of the trial. It was Sarah who offered an opinion.

"Do you know why the judge gave the careless driving decision?"

"Tell me."

"If there ever was a trial where there was ample evidence to demonstrate dangerous driving, this was it. But a conviction on that charge would run the risk of an appeal. Mind you, the brother would have to be willing to throw away another $200,000 on his loser of a brother, but it was a risk the judge didn't want to take. Convicting him of careless driving got rid of that risk, and the judge could still give Abbott the maximum sentence of six months in jail plus the loss of his licence for five years.

"It's probably all he would have got even if he was convicted of dangerous driving. The public doesn't know the difference between the two charges. All they see is a six-month sentence, and that will satisfy them. It's a win—win for the judge: no appeal. And the public will believe that justice has been done because Abbott has been sent to jail."

"You don't think he got off because Underhill came from a prestigious law firm?"

"Maybe, but I know Judge Taylor pretty well, and he's not likely to be influenced by things like that."

"You sure got Abbott in the cross-examination," said Mariner.

Sarah smiled. She liked the praise from someone with experience.

"I still think it should have been second-degree murder," he continued. "Abbott tried to kill or injure Spider. There was intent. But perhaps you were right. We could never have got a conviction on that charge."

She smiled. "But on the other hand, if we had stuck with second-degree murder, maybe the judge would have reduced it to dangerous driving. Who knows? You take your chances and have to live with the outcome."

The conversation drifted on to other, more personal things. Sarah was single. "No time in this job for marriage or kids," she admitted.

Mariner made his own confession. "Married twice, with all the scars to prove it. It's hard to do this type of work and have the emotional energy left to hold a marriage together."

Sarah liked that. For those who took it seriously, this type of work took enormous commitment, and there was little left over for something as intense as a close relationship.

As the evening wore on, the attraction between them grew stronger. Neither of them wanted to break the spell and so they sat over their coffee and then a drink. Mariner waited for the invitation to be offered and finally it came.

"I just live down on the waterfront," Sarah said as casually as she could make it. "Would you like to come for a drink?"

"I'd like that very much."

As they walked down to Queen's Quay and Sarah's condo, they both knew what was about to happen. They felt anxious. Things had never gone well for either of them in relationships, but they were eager for it at the same time.

The next morning Mariner woke up around eight. The sun had just broken the horizon and flooded the bedroom of Sarah's apartment. He got out of bed and stood at the window of the living room that went from floor to ceiling.

The harbour lay almost at his feet. Beyond that were the Toronto Islands, and then the blue of Lake Ontario sparkling in the bright sunlight of a beautiful day. As the sun warmed his body, he thought about the last chore he had to do to complete his work on the Shelly McTavish case.

They left early, walking together up York Street to Queen. Then Sarah went east to the courts in Old City Hall, while Mariner walked north to Dundas and the 52

Division police station. On the way he paused to buy a *Toronto Star.*

When he got to the station he spread the paper out on his desk. On page three was the account of the trial. The reporter got most of it right, but he missed the nuance of the cross-examinations. What Mariner liked most of all was the large photo of Spider and his girlfriend, Jay. Over the picture of the handsome, young couple was the headline: "Fighting for Safe Streets for Cyclists." The detective smiled. At least one good thing had come out of this tragic case.

Mariner phoned his friend Bob Thurston, the personal injury lawyer, and at about 10 that morning, he took one of the unmarked police cars and drove into the west end. He knew he was not supposed to do this. It was against police policy to advise anyone on civil cases, but he didn't care. This one was different.

The apartment was on a quiet residential street. Mariner parked and walked to the low-rise, older apartment building. He found the door he was looking for and knocked. As he waited, he thought he heard the sounds of a baby, and when the door opened The Hawk was standing there holding Baby Marilyn in his arms.

"Yes?" The Hawk asked. He knew this man dressed in a rumpled suit was familiar, but he couldn't place him.

"I'm Detective Mariner, who worked on your wife's case."

"What do you want?" The Hawk was suspicious. Police never brought good news.

"May I come in?"

For a moment The Hawk was tempted to say no, but he relented.

The room was a large, open space. Doors to a bedroom and bath were on one side. North-facing windows let in warm, diffuse sunlight. A table was set up close to the open kitchen. It was covered with materials of a work in progress. A baby's bed and playpen were in one corner and toys were scattered about on the floor.

"What is it?" Hawk demanded, his voice betraying his unease.

"Yesterday the court heard the case of Charles Abbott, who drove the car that killed your wife, Shelly. He was convicted of careless driving, sentenced to six months in jail, and he lost his licence for five years."

"Yeah?" said The Hawk passively. He had not gone to the trial. It was too painful.

Mariner studied him. He was pale, diminished even, from the time he had last seen him at the scene of the accident. "I thought that you would want to know."

"What difference does it make?"

"It makes a lot of difference."

"It won't bring Shelly back."

"That's true. A lot of people are upset about that."

Hawk shrugged. He had put Baby Marilyn into her playpen and came back to sit on a straight-backed chair. Mariner was still standing. Hawk's sadness felt oppressive.

"You must feel overwhelmed by everything that has happened," Mariner offered.

"Overwhelmed?" The Hawk looked up at the detective. "Sick, angry.... It's not fuckin' fair."

"No, it's not fair. You're right. A lot of things are not fair in life."

"People don't understand," he said quietly. "It's not just our lives together. She believed in me. I try to work but I can't."

"But you have to carry on, Hawk. You have no other choice."

"Don't call me Hawk. I'm not The Hawk anymore. I am Sam. Samuel Dockstader. That's all. Sam—never The Hawk again."

"But that's not true."

"What do you know?"

"Your friends and Shelly's friends still call you The Hawk."

"I don't feel like it."

"They believe in you. To them you have the passion and drive of a hawk."

"You mean Derrick."

"Yes, and others." Mariner was stretching the truth, but this was important. "They want you to be The Hawk because they see that you have the vision and talent to be something special."

Hawk was crying now. "They don't know anything about me. Only Shelly understood." It was all too much. The truth was that he didn't believe in himself anymore. Why was this stranger, this detective, dragging this out of him? He just wanted to be left alone.

"One thing I do know is that Shelly believed in you," said Mariner. "I never met her, but she must have believed in you because she sacrificed her own art and went out to work so you could have time to develop your talent."

"And that's why she died."

"No. What happened was tragic. It could have happened to anyone."

"But it didn't. It happened to Shelly."

"That can't be changed. That's the tragedy you have to live with. But always remember, she had a dream for you. For her, you are The Hawk. That is fixed in time and will never change."

For the longest time they said nothing. The Hawk stared at the floor thinking about these words. Yes, Shelly believed in him and no matter what happened that would always be there. Finally he looked up at Mariner.

The detective reached into his pocket and drew out a business card. He stepped across the distance between them and handed it to The Hawk.

"This is the card of a lawyer I know, Bob Thurston. He is expecting your call. Yesterday Abbott was found guilty of careless driving in the death of Shelly. That means that the court—the legal system—has found him responsible for her death, and that means that his insurance company is obliged to pay you for that loss. Bob Thurston will get you that money. I don't know how much—$1 million, maybe more. Bob will know. He's the best in the business. Don't be greedy, but take it and spend it wisely. Think of it as Shelly's final gift to you."

The Hawk was studying him closely.

"Remember this," Mariner continued. "She believed in you and now you have to return the confidence that she had in you." He paused. Mariner had gone far beyond what policemen are supposed to do. "Promise me that you will phone Bob Thurston when I leave."

Hawk looked at him and then at the business card. Who was this policeman and why was he doing this for him?

"Promise you will do it this morning," Mariner repeated.

The Hawk nodded. "I'll do it for Shelly and … and Baby Marilyn."

"And for yourself."

Mariner went to the door, and as he was easing his way out he glanced back. The Hawk was studying the card with his quiet intensity.

16082400R00091

Made in the USA
Charleston, SC
04 December 2012